T0102888

Pindi Calling

Irfan Haq

Order this book online at www.trafford.com
or email orders@trafford.com

Most Trafford titles are also available at major online book retailers.

Note for Librarians: A cataloguing record for this book is available from Library and Archives Canada at www.collectionscanada.ca/amicus/index-e.html

Printed in Victoria, BC, Canada.

ISBN: 978-1-4269-1364-8 (Soft)

We at Trafford believe that it is the responsibility of us all, as both individuals and corporations, to make choices that are environmentally and socially sound. You, in turn, are supporting this responsible conduct each time you purchase a Trafford book, or make use of our publishing services. To find out how you are helping, please visit www.trafford.com/responsiblepublishing.html

Our mission is to efficiently provide the world's finest, most comprehensive book publishing service, enabling every author to experience success. To find out how to publish your book, your way, and have it available worldwide, visit us online at www.trafford.com

Trafford rev. 07/15/2009

Trafford PUBLISHING® www.trafford.com

North America & international
toll-free: 1 888 232 4444 (USA & Canada)
phone: 250 383 6864 • fax: 250 383 6804 • email: info@trafford.com

"FOR MY AMI AND ALL THOSE WHO
BELIEVED IN ME, I HOPE THIS PROVES YOU RIGHT.
AND TO ALL THOSE WHO
GAVE UP ON ME, I HOPE IT PROVES YOU WRONG."

Chapter 1

"Can I get change? Five singles?" I said, putting a five down on the bar and realizing my mistake.

Josh would never give me five singles because he knew where they were headed. I should have bought another drink or something to get those singles.

"No, I am sorry," was the response that I knew was coming. "I am really low on singles," Josh said fumbling with the remote.

He was looking for some dirty movie on his dish setup since it was only four guys sitting in the bar. There were no females that could be offended.

"Come on," I insisted, "there has to be some singles in that register of yours. How about that bucket you got hanging over there for the tips. Don't tell me all your tips are big bills."

"What are you, fucking deaf? I told you; I don't have any singles. And I need the ones I have."

"Okay then," I said, deciding to change my strategy. "I want another shot. Black Haus."

Josh gave me a quick glance.

"First of all, we know your pussy-ass can't handle anything besides your usual shit. But if you really want it, I will buy it for ya' since you are such a regular."

At this point, Joe, one of the other guys at the other end of the bar spoke up, "You need singles? I got 'em."

"No, don't give him any fucking singles," shouted Josh. "He's gonna go play the jukebox, and it'll be the same shit he plays every other night. His U2 and shit. I can't stand that Bono's voice anymore."

Now keep in mind that when he said Bono, he did not say it the way it is correctly pronounced. Instead, he said it like "Sonny Bono's" last name. So now, he was insulting my favorite artist on top of not letting me play my music.

"What do you have against them? They are not bad," Joey inquired, further fanning the flames.

"No, they were… not bad. But when you have to be here and listen to that shit over and over, it gets to you. Why don't I ask the jukebox guy to take it out? Well, I did. But the guy said he can't because that cd is the most played. Thanks in large part to this asshole, who's got this obsession with Bono. And no, he can't play anything different from them. Its the same friggin' songs, over and over. 'All I Want is You', or some shit like that. Call me a bad businessman, but I am a human first. Enough of that shit."

"Okay, then," I tried again, "I want to buy Joe a drink. What are you having, Joey?"

"No, Joey's not gonna have another drink unless your ass is driving his home," Josh replied. "And, no, you are not getting a bag of popcorn or beef jerky or any shit that's gonna end up in the garbage and put a couple of singles in your hand."

"Fine," I said getting up and walking to the door. "And, by the way, I am going back."

"Back to school? Back to your house?"

"No, I am going back to Pakistan," I said, slamming the door behind me.

What just happened? A lot, actually. I said farewell to the bar I had been calling home for the past couple of years. The name of the place was Josh's Pub, on the corner of Colbert and Henders in the small hamlet of Kinsville, New Jersey. It was a little dive bar. I ended up being a regular there after a couple of friends from high school showed me the way there. No, I didn't become some flaming drunk, even though I was there almost every night of the week. But I never did drink too much. Just my usual bottle of Molson Ice and a shot of Rumple Minze. That was it... just enough to get a buzz. But smoked a lot sitting there. Had those two drinks but went through almost a half a pack in that duration. Never strayed from my usual drinks though. Never got drunk. Oh, they tried. Friends, including Josh would buy me shit to just see me drunk but it never worked. Never got drunk. I liked staying in control.

I saw friends get hammered, trying to get me hammered.... and I ended up driving them home.

Anyway, like I was just saying, it was a little dive bar in a little town. Mostly a local hangout. Never saw more than five people there during the week. Weekends got a little busier. Of course, the busiest time of the year was Thanksgiving weekend when it was tough to even move around in the place since everybody came with their visiting family members, hoping to make them more bearable.

I mean, there were people that I would only see once a year. But I only went there for a couple of years so there were people I only saw twice in my life.

But getting back to what it was all about, Josh's Pub was a little place. If you were there and, God forbid, there was an emergency, it would probably take you a lot longer to figure out which way to exit than it would take you to actually exit. There was the back door going out to the parking lot and the front door leading to the street.

Josh originally wanted to call the place Josh's. He was cheap and wanted to spend as little as possible on the sign. When the landlord told him that he should elaborate a bit, he added "Pub". Simple.

Inside, there were about fifteen stools at the bar, a couple of tables to the sides, if you wanted to sit there, five TVs behind the bar, a pool table, jukebox, and a couple of video game machines.

And one thing that I always thought should not be in a bar... a dartboard. If you were going to give intoxicated folks a dartboard, it should be one of those Nerf-jobs since pointy sharp objects in one hand and a beer in the other just doesn't seem safe to me. But then, I don't own and operate a bar. However, moving on beyond the inner geography of the bar, there isn't much else to talk about regarding the matter.

The owner, Joshua Harmon, was a small Italian guy in his early thirties. Actually, he co- owned the bar with his friend, Jim, and wife, Diane. They all took turns running the place. Except that, Diane was usually at her other job, working for one of the many banks in town. Yes, it was a small town (a little over one square mile) but there were something like three banks. So you would think that the town had a lot of money. Not really. It was your typical blue collar town with the majority of people in some kind of construction or landscaping job.

When winter came, the landscapers turned into snow-plowers and the construction people went into hibernation.

Like I said before, it was your typical local dive bar, except on the weekends and holidays. It was the same people you would see every day, getting together after work to ease their tensions, unload their woes, and bullshit about everything and nothing at all. Racially, everyone in the establishment was either Irish or Italian. Pretty much, like the town. This is where I was the oddball. I, like I hinted at earlier, was from Pakistan. How did I end up in this crowd of white people? That's a whole different story, though not a long one. I went to high school in the neighboring town of Ridgewood, which was just about the same in its ethnic makeup. (Actually, it was a bit different since there was a large Indian community there besides the ruling class of Italians.)

For some reason, when I went to school there, I didn't have any friends that were Indian. I hardly knew any Indian kids. All my friends *ended up* being *white guys*. No, it had nothing to do with the tensions between India and Pakistan. I never went out to choose friends. Friendship just ends up happening and in my case it happened with those guys.

Anyway, I am supposed to be telling you about how I ended up being a regular at Josh's Pub. Well, it was a couple of friends from high school, that turned me onto the place. They left, I stayed. And I was never treated any different. I was one of them... just as Irish and Italian as some of the old timers that had been calling the place home for a lot longer, because the bar had been there for quite a long time. It used to be run by Josh's parents and after their passing had become the responsibility of their only son.

I must have a lot of heart for the place since that is all I have been talking about.

Yes, I did love the place but I should divulge a little bit of information about myself.

Chapter 2

My name is Irfan Haq.

Actually it was Irfan Ul Haq. Is Ul my middle name? No, that's where things get a little mixed up.

I will use the same example that I have been using to explain this to so many people. Ul is just a bridge that connects the first name to the last. Kind of like "De la" in Oscar de la Hoya.

Would "de la" be a middle name? No. And that is what the "Ul" in my name is. However, somewhere along the way, it lost its original purpose and my name ended up becoming Irfan U Haq. And then just Irfan Haq.

I was born in 1978 in Holy Family Hospital in Rawalpindi, Pakistan. I was a C-section baby and as I tell people, I was forced into coming into this world. I went to school in Pakistan until eighth grade. Then I was sent to the United States for better education since the education system back there was terrible.

My father, Imran ul Haq, worked for Habib Bank, one of the few large banks in Pakistan. I think he was a Bank Manager or something. I never really paid too much attention; we were never that close. I was an only child and according to my own parents, I wasn't spoiled at all.

My mother was what most women in Pakistan was at the time... a housewife, concentrating on raising a good child. Her name, by the way, was Nabeela. My father had another brother who had moved to the US back in the late 1970's. He was an older brother, but there was the oldest brother, Zain. He was still in Pakistan and was actually my favorite uncle. Taya Ji, I called him. Because that is who he was - my "taya." You see, things are not that simple in Pakistani culture.

Each person has their own title. Not all uncles are called uncle and not all aunts are called aunt. A father's older brothers are "tayas" while the younger brothers are "chachas." The sisters of the father are "phuphis." Meanwhile, the mother's brothers are "mamoon" and the mother's sisters are "khala."

A little confusing, isn't it? So I won't even get into the in-laws and how each one gets their own name. Husband's older brother, younger brother, and sisters. Wife's siblings. All have their own name. But I just thought that I would talk a little bit about it to illustrate the kind of complexities I faced as a child.

No, I am just kidding. It was all good.

Anyway, back in 1991, I was sent to the US to live with my younger taya and his wife. They didn't have any kids of their own and guiding me to a better educational frontier became their new job.

So 1991 is when I permanently set foot in the US. At least that is what was intended by all involved, including myself. I started at Ridgewood High in the ninth grade. My first day of school, I was put in ESL since I was a fresh arrival. And on top of that I didn't talk too much which the guidance counselor thought was because of a language barrier that I had not yet fathomed. Well, it was actually because I didn't have much to say. That plus the fear that only a newly arrived immigrant would know. Years later, when I would read Stranger in a Strange Land, the title would be something I could relate to the most.

But getting back to starting school, I was put in ESL (English as a Second Language).

I couldn't argue with that since it sure was a second language. Actually a third, if you wanted to get technical since Urdu was my native language but I had grown up in a household that mainly communicated in Punjabi.

That was one of the many dialects of Pakistan that I didn't really speak but understood. Why didn't I speak it? Because I didn't like the way it sounded. I had already told my family that and they weren't too happy about it but adjusted to it.

In 1987, I came to the US for a visit. In 1989, I came for another visit. In 1991, I moved here.

And in 1998, I left.

But getting back to my first day of school. So, I was put in ESL. The second day, I was put in Honors English because apparently, I was fine in English.

"Why did Mrs. Wilson feel the need to put you in ESL? You are reading this book and you seem to understand everything," said Mrs. Warren, the ESL teacher.

I was reading a Tom Clancy novel at the time, which I turned to that first day, since I had dropped in mid-term and the rest of the class was taking a test. I was told to sit aside and kill some time however I found it suitable. And that is when I decided to pick up where I had left off in *The Cardinal of the Kremlin.*

"Why didn't you tell her that you shouldn't be in ESL?" was the next question. My straight-faced response, "Because she didn't ask and I figured I could do really well if I just played along."

"Now that is not fair to these other kids and even for you," I was told.

So back to the counselor I went and my unintentional charade ended.

Then it was off to Honors English.

A stranger in a stranger land.

Chapter 3

"Ten thousand spoons when all you need is a knife."

That is not ironic. Its messed up, but sure as hell not ironic. But that is what Alanis Morrisette sang, sold, and which millions heard and bought. What is ironic is what happened to me. One of the greatest fears that a Pakistani parent faces when sending a child to the US is that the kid will end up marrying some American girl. After all, there have been plenty who did that. But a lot of times, these people would marry some American girl to get legal status since they had gotten to the US illegally. But I was fine and legal. I came with a green card which I had gotten since my taya who was living here had sponsored my whole family as soon as he became a citizen.

Still there was a maternal fear... what if some white witch traps my son? They are not faithful. They don't make good mothers. Or even worse, what if my son marries some black girl? That would be the end of it. I never understood the prejudices my people had against black people. Remember that I was not from Ireland. I was from Pakistan where people tended to be of a darker shade. But Pakistan is full of a lot of internal hate. Americans live here and try to unite a nation of people who look different. Pakistanis (that is what people from Pakistan are and not Pakistanians) all look pretty much alike in terms of skin. But still they find reasons to hate each other. The country is Muslim, but there is hatred among the different sects of Muslims. You can be of the same sect and still find reasons to hate each other.

How?

Well it could be the language you speak. Urdu is the national language but there are so many dialects. So now you have people who fight each other because of the dialect spoken. And you have the Shiites who don't like the Sunnis. And you have the Punjabis who don't like the Sindhis.

But that is where I grew up. That is what made me. That is what defined me.

But getting back to my ironic life. There I was growing up in the US, surrounded by American girls, but falling in love with a Pakistani girl and getting my heart broken by a Pakistani girl. Maybe mom should have let me take a chance with some *white witch* who was expected to be unfaithful.

Chapter 4

"You know what would have helped?" said Mike putting down his bottle of Coors Light.

"No," I replied taking a drag off of my cigarette and putting my glass down.

"If your name was Ronnie," was the response.

"And how the fuck would that have been helpful? Whichever case you are talking about," I said back.

"Wasn't that Maria's last name? "Do Ronnie" or some shit like that?", he said.

ॐ

What is going on, you are probably saying. I was just talking about Pakistan and now I am in some bar. Well, life happens in a certain pattern. You are born...you grow old...and then you die. But looking back at life, you don't remember it in any order. This book is about my life and I am just putting it down as it happens in my head. So, no, there isn't a straightforward pattern.

ॐ

Remember when Pulp Fiction first came out? Everyone hailed Tarantino as a genius for jumbling up the course of events.

I didn't think too much of it. But now I am doing the same.

This happened at Josh's Pub around 1998 or so.

ॐ

Anyway, Mike was a little confused. Maybe it was the alcohol starting to talk since it wasn't his first bottle that he had just put down.

"First of all, her name is not Maria. It's Maryah. Remember that she is from Pakistan. Second, her last name is Durani, not "Do Ronnie". That is a pretty common name in Pakistan, I think," I explained to my friend even though I wasn't sure all of it registered because he would be asking the same question a couple of nights later.

But what was he talking about? Remember I said that I fell for a Pakistani girl. Well, that was her. Maryah Durani. And this was the exact place where I met her. Josh's Pub. How that happened was a major part of how I became such a huge fan of U2. You will wonder why when I give out some more details.

Chapter 5

Josh's Pub was on MLK Avenue which was pretty much the biggest road going through town.

And that was a pretty strange name for a road in Kinsville. Why? Because it was one of the whitest towns in New Jersey. Actually, let me correct myself. It was a white town. I don't think there was a single black family living there. It would be an ideal place for someone from Pakistan because I had learned that Pakistanis avoided places that were not generally populated by white people. Strange since Pakistanis don't tend to be too white. (Unless you are talking about the Pathans from the northern part of Pakistan who are pretty white skinned.)

Anyway, what I was trying to say is that it was odd for a town like Kinsville to have a MLK Avenue running through its center. And it was even stranger for a person like myself to walk into and start calling a place like JP's my watering hole. But I was treated just as anybody else. Those people became good friends and ended up being more offended when I referred to myself as a "sand nigger."

But that is how things happened. No wonder I thought of the place as my home away from home.

I heard somewhere that your birthplace is actually where you find out who you are. So, in a way, Josh's Pub was my birthplace. In other words, I loved it there. It may make me sound like an alcoholic but there was more to it than just the booze. It was about being in the company of friends and bullshitting about nothing at all. It was about talking problems like you were going to solve them and realizing that you had just killed an hour without doing shit. It was about shooting a game of pool and forgetting halfway through if you were the high ball or low.

And let's not forget the music. Putting money in the jukebox to hear music that you had gotten sick of listening to on the radio. That is how it was. And that is why I loved it. Plus there was that buzz you got after downing a few too many. It was all good.

It was late 1997 when I met the love of my life in that bar. Did I mention before that it was ironic?

Chapter 6

The guy moved from Pakistan and became a fucking drunk. That is what you are probably thinking. And it might be justified since that is pretty much what I have been talking about. Life at Josh's Pub. But I did mention earlier that I was going to jump around in the story of my life. And I think it is time to change up the monotony of my ode.

I also mentioned earlier that my father had an older brother who had chosen to stay in Pakistan. My favorite uncle; Taya Ji. He lived a simple life. Kind of like the Walden of Pakistan. A hippie-ish existence. A simple life.

Never married and living solo in Rawalpindi, which was the next city over from Islamabad, the country's capital. So simple that he did not even own a car. He was happy with his Sohrab bicycle.

By the way, Sohrab was a Pakistani bicycle company. He didn't even want to support any foreign bike manufacturers. But his brothers had eventually convinced him to upgrade a little. He didn't want a car because he didn't know how to drive. So he settled for a motorcycle. Kind of.

He ended up getting a Wespa motor scooter, which his brothers paid for since he didn't have much money, either. He lived in a tiny one bedroom apartment, without any air conditioning, just a ceiling fan. But what he did, was the best profession in my eyes.

He had a little desk set up at the Rawalpindi Train Station. That is where he read and wrote letters for people. Literacy wasn't too high in Pakistan. And there were a lot of people who couldn't read or write. That is where he came in. He had gotten his education in Pakistan, unlike his brothers who had gone abroad to pursue their education. But he was a loyal Pakistani. He went to school in Pakistan and even went to some college. Then he dropped out and set his table at the train station. Like I just mentioned, that is where he carried on his work. According to him, it wasn't about the few Rupees he got. It was more about helping out the people. People that he saw as in need of someone like him.

So the people would bring him letters that they got, often from relatives living abroad. He would read them and tell them how their families were doing. And then people would have him write letters to their loved ones. Sons and daughters who had ventured beyond the borders in pursuit of a better future. And he wouldn't charge the people a fee. They could give him whatever they thought worthy or could afford. It was their choice. Sometimes people would give him nothing because that is what they had. But they gave him their blessings and said that Allah would reward him. Or they said they would pay him as soon as they got some money. He never coaxed them into finding a way for a payback. Their prayers and blessings were enough.

Yes, that is why Taya Ji was such a great man in my eyes. A simple man. The kind of person that the country needed more of...

Chapter 7

I know that I mentioned earlier that this is not a straightforward tome. I jump around a lot. I was just talking about Pakistan and my Taya Ji. But I think I will return to Josh's Pub once again.

And I shall do so many more times because a lot happened there. Life happened there.

In case you are doing the math in your head, you are absolutely right.

I was not twenty one when I started going there. So how could I be drinking at the time? To put it simply, I knew people. Josh knew I wasn't even twenty. But he served me, anyway. Because I had known him for a while before I became a patron at his establishment.

Kinsville, like I said before, was a small town. Barely a square mile. The Pub was on MLK Boulevard. A couple of blocks away was my place of employment, a small convenience store called The Stop and Save Mart.

That name was half right because you did have to stop. Saving was another case, but the prices were pretty close to what those kinds of stores charged. Couldn't compete with the big supermarkets but saving money wasn't the object there. People stopped in there for quickies. Stop in to get whatever, not wait in a long line, and walk out in a fraction of the time it would take you in a supermarket. The place was owned and run by Mr. and Mrs. Patel. Yes, they were Indians. So how did I land a job in that place?

Well, I used to stop in there for cigarettes all the time. They knew who I was. And whenever I was there I started talking to the couple in Hindi. The thing is that Hindi is spoken just like Urdu, which was my native language. It is written completely differently but spoken the same. Which is a big reason why Indian movies are so popular in Pakistan. Yes, India and Pakistan may be sworn enemies but Indian movies do better in Pakistan than Pakistani movies.

But getting back to my employment at the Patel's.

One day, I just asked Mr. Patel if he wanted to hire me as a cashier or whatever.

Money was the problem, according to him, and business was slow. In other words, he didn't trust someone outside of the family to be behind his cash register.

I told him that he could pay me whatever he thought was suitable and that I could be trusted. Never stole a penny in my entire life, I told him and I wasn't lying. He said he would discuss it with his wife and tell me in a couple of days.

A couple of days later he said that I could work there because his wife thought it would be a good idea to have me behind the counter. My English was flawless and accent free. Theirs wasn't so perfect and they did have that thick accent. Kind of like Apu from The Simpson's. Plus I could deal better with the Americans since I seemed to be pretty Americanized.

Anyway, that is where I knew Josh from. He used to stop in there and he knew who I was when I first set foot in his bar. He knew I wasn't 21 but chose to serve me since it would have been awkward if he didn't and we ran into each other again at the store. At least that is how I justified it for myself.

And thus began my drinking career at nineteen years of age.

By the way, the town police station was also a block away from the store so I knew most of the cops… and that helped. Cops were part of the regular flow of customers and I got to know them. That was another culture shock for me. Back in Pakistan, the police had to be one of the most corrupt group of professionals around.

If you were unlucky enough to own any sort of establishment in their vicinity, then God help you.

They would stop in and demand you give them your services for free. Actually, pay them if you wanted any sort of protection from criminals. And if there weren't any criminals then there were going to be plenty if you didn't take care of the police.

In the US, it wasn't so. The cops would stop in and pay for each and every item they got. If you tried to let them go without paying, they insisted that you charge them. Anyway, I got to be friends with a lot of these cops and they ended up being drinking buddies on quite a few occasions.

So working at that store expanded my social circle and put some money in my pocket. Things were looking good.

Chapter 8

I mentioned earlier how I was a huge fan of the rock band U2. Actually, I'm a big fan of music, period.

I never really got into Pakistani music, even when I was living there. In the US, I ended up spending whatever little money I had on buying cds and never really got into whatever was popular at the time. Thank God, actually. Because when I moved to the US in 1991, music that was popular was not going to last, in my opinion. MC Hammer, Vanilla Ice, and their likes were heard blaring out of cars passing by. Not my type of thing. Remember Kriss Kross? I do, and I didn't like it then or now. I was just a rock 'n roll type of guy. So how did I become a big fan of U2? Always did like them but 1997ensured their place in my music library as the greatest rock band ever.

I also mentioned how my friends didn't understand why I actually liked them. This is how that story happened. The year 1997 is when U2 released Pop and went on a worldwide PopMart tour. Did I go see them? No. Actually, I have never been to a live concert in my entire life.

I was sitting at Josh's Pub in my usual seat one night. About halfway down the bar, far enough from the pool table so I wouldn't be constantly bothered by someone trying to make a shot with my back getting in their way. Two girls walked in through the front door, which was a little rare, since it was mostly guys hanging out at the bar.. and no, it wasn't a gay bar. It was just a dude type of place. Remember The Blue Oyster from those Police Academy movies? Of course, you don't. Well this was not that type of hang out for guys. Anyway, these girls ended up sitting a couple of stools away from me. I was sitting there sipping my shot of RumpleMinze and smoking my cigarette. Sipping a shot? Well, I never liked those dinky shot glasses. I always told whoever was working to put my double shot in a rocks glass but hold back on the rocks. So what was stranger about these two girls was the fact that they were not white. My first guess would have been Indian or maybe even Pakistani.

As I would soon find out, it was the later.

They just each ordered a bottle of Coors Light. I signaled Josh to take it out of my money lying on the bar.

"Oh, Irfan's gonna buy a drink for his kind," said Josh in a low voice as he took a ten off my money.

I just smirked a 'yup.'

"Thank you," the two girls said in unison as Josh let them know I had just bought them the drinks.

"No problem," I said and added, "I haven't seen you before."

"Well, actually we were just passing through and thought we'd cool off a bit," replied the older-looking one.

"And I am not from around here so I just tag along with wherever she takes me," said the other one pointing to her friend.

Their English was good; pretty perfect actually. There was the accent though; a Pakistani accent. Once again, not like Apu from the Simpson's, but an accent that was not American. Besides, everyone has an accent.

I know that this may sound like a line that has been used countless times in movies, but it is actually what I said.

"You two seem to be new around here."

The one that seemed like she was the older one of the two replied with a brief nod.

She picked up her bottle, took a couple of sips, and then decided that she should elaborate a bit. After all, I did just buy them the drinks. And I didn't seem like a threatening type; at least I hoped so.

"Actually I live a couple of towns away. My friend here, though, is not even close to being close by."

I may have mentioned this earlier but her English had a certain accent to it. Not too ethnic, but just not American.

"Now don't take this the wrong way but you are either Indian or Pakistani," I said.

"Actually, we are from Pakistan," she replied.

"Then let me just say from personal experience that having a beer is not really a traditional Pakistani activity.

Muslim?" I inquired.

"Yeah, I guess," she replied a little embarrassingly.

"Well, don't worry because I also happen to be from Pakistan. But in terms of religion, I just say that I am from a Muslim family. Leaves it open for interpretation," I said.

"Really?" she said.

I just nodded. Through this whole exchange, the other girl had just sat there, sipping the beer, looking around, and nodding on occasion.

She was the one who had my attention, which I hoped, wasn't too obvious.

Pretty and thin along the lines of Kate Moss, she had a certain look that just caught your attention.

"My name is Irfan, by the way," I said extending my hand.

The one I had been talking to shook my hand saying, "I am Shazia, and this quiet is my bestest friend, Marya."

Yes, Marya. From my earlier revelations, can you guess where this is headed?

Chapter 9

And that was about the gist of the conversation we had at the bar.

After the introductions, we went back to being our quiet selves. The two girls were talking.

I couldn't hear them over the jukebox which was blaring some crap that one of the other regulars had managed to play.

Managed? Because when the guy had gone up to the jukebox, he had *had a few* already and was struggling to get his dollar bill in the slot. But he had managed and ended up playing Low Rider as his opening selection. What else did he play?

I wouldn't know because it was my time to leave. I finished my remaining RumpleMinze, picked up my pack of cigarettes, left whatever singles were sitting on the bar for Josh, and headed towards the door.

I think I was his best tipper. Three or four dollars after my usual two drinks. I think that worked out to a pretty good average.

Anyway, I had to say bye to the two girls.

"Well, ladies, I am done for the night," I said. "But I am heading over to the diner on Route 22, if you would like to join me there?"

"I don't know. It's getting kinda late, but which diner?" asked Shazia.

"I just told you, The Diner," I said. "That's what the place is called. The Diner. It's in the center aisle of Rt. 22, if you turn left at this light up here and go all the way down until you hit 22 east. Then just make the first U-turn, head west, and its about a quarter of a mile down."

"Well, we'll see but it was nice meeting you," Shazia said and Maryah nodded in agreement.

I walked out, got into my car and drove off.

ॐ

It was the usual people working at the diner. Just a couple of waitresses, the guy handing out the menus at the front, and that's about it. Keep in mind that this was a 24-hour diner, and at this time, 11:45 pm, was usually pretty empty.

"There's my favorite late night customer," said Carla, the heavy set waitress who always got to wait on me at this hour. "Smoking, right honey?"

"Yup, mama didn't raise no quitter, Carly," I replied.

"You wanna sit at the counter since its just you?" she asked.

"I think I will take a table tonight," I replied, not knowing why I had just chosen to sit at a table by myself.

I got a table about halfway down the middle. I sat down and lit a cigarette, of course.

"You want the menu or are you just gonna have your usual?" Carla asked.

"Just the usual," I replied.

My usual was french fries and a slice of chocolate cheese cake. And, no, I wasn't fat. I was around a 155 pounds at 5'10". Not bad.

My food came and I started on my fries. Slowly at first and slower later on.

A couple of fries later, I heard the door open. I turned around to see who came in. I wasn't totally surprised to see Shazia and Marya walking in. I sort of knew they would come. On the other hand, maybe I was a believer that if you hoped for something hard enough, it would happen.

And it just did. And it's a good thing I was sitting at a table.

Chapter 10

"You look like a fakir," Taya Ji said as I stepped out of the taxi.

I took my bags out, gave the driver the money and looked at Taya Ji.

"You remember what a fakir is? Actually some of the fakirs I have seen dress better than you. Look at that," he continued, "your jeans have holes in them, you have a beard, and you look like you haven't shaved in God knows how long. Is that what America makes you?"

"Well, it's nice to see you too Taya Ji," I replied, smiling. I hadn't seen him in over ten years but he was still the same. Always critical of how you looked. Wanted everybody to be dressed like they were going to a big business meeting. He was just as I last remembered him. Skinny, tall, and dressed in his favorite type of clothing. Shalwar kameez. How could people wear these pants and still breathe? That was his outlook on a wardrobe that had even caught on in Pakistan. First it was just guys but now you could even see women wearing jeans.

At least the modern ones, as they were looked at as being.

"You know, those clothes are no good for the body. They don't allow proper circulation," he said stepping forward and giving me a hearty hug.

The guy was alright. A little bitter at times maybe but alright in my book. The best uncle I had.

"I hope you will be okay since I don't have an A.C. Just a fan. But sometimes not even that because the power goes out a lot.

Load Shedding they call it. Make the poor people suffer so the rich can keep enjoying their Air Conditioners."

"I will be fine, taya ji. America makes you tough," I said.

Then we stepped inside his living quarters. No carpet, bare walls, a window facing the road, and a ceiling fan running on what I figured was low but would turn out to be high. And a wooden bed on one side of the room with ropes holding it together and a squished pillow at one end.

"You take the bed. I will put a sheet on the floor," he said.

"Never," I said. "I could never lie on a place higher than yours."

"At least you are still humble," he said. "The toilet is over there.

There is no shower. There is a bucket in there, just fill it up and take a bath when you feel like it."

"With this heat, I think I will take quite a few of them," I said. "By the way, where's the kitchen?"

"Kitchen?" he said with smirk. "There is no kitchen. My kitchen is on the corner over there. I just go to Khan's Canteen when I want something. Best cook around."

"That will be fine with me then," I said sitting down on the squeaking bed with a little apprehension that the thing might break under my much heavier body.

Yes, I was a man of my word. When I told the people back at Josh's Pub that I was going back to Pakistan, I had meant it. It hadn't been the alcohol talking.

"Are you sure you want to stay here?" Taya Ji asked. "I mean if you want to move back to Pakistan, you can stay with your parents. They have a nice place," he suggested.

"No, I am sure I want to be here."

After an absence of around eight years, I was back to where I had started.

At least, close to it.

By the way, fakirs were the beggars you ran into all around. Begging for money, food, or whatever could be spared. Yes, I was home.

Chapter 11

I got up out of my seat and waved to the girls to let them know where I was. So I didn't get up all the way but my ass did leave the cushion. And in my world that is getting up.

They smiled and waved back, acknowledging my effort. They sat in the seats across from me with a table, which could have been a continent, separating us.

"So you came," I said.

"No, we got lost and just stopped in to get directions," replied Shazia with a smirk.

"Whatever," I said rolling my eyes. "And how are you, missy?" I asked looking at Marya.

"Ok, I guess. Just a little buzzed. Not hammered, obviously," came the reply.

She had a low voice. Almost like she was a shy one. But, obviously, the girl had some spirit if she had managed to come a million miles away from her home in Pakistan. Not many parents, would let their girls go like that.

"Anyway, do you ladies want something to eat? Drink? Non-alcoholic, of course," I asked.

"My treat," I elaborated.

"No, I don't think so," said Shazia. "Unless, tubby here wants something?"

"No, I am good," said Marya.

"Well, you have to get something. This place is not a shelter," I said.

"Just coffees, then, I guess," Shazia said. "Black. And you?" she asked Marya.

"Same," was all she said.

I called Carly over and gave her the additions.

"Alrighty, stud," she said with a smile and walked over to the coffee station. She came back, put two cups in front of the girls, and filled them up. "Refills are free, and all the crap you need to make them bearable is on the table," she said walking away.

"Carly hates coffee," I explained. "She says that she used to like it but has had enough of it just serving it to people. Says she finds the smell nauseating now."

The girls nodded and went to work on their coffees. Shazia just took a sip, burned her lip, and put the cup down to let it cool off for a while. Marya put a little milk in hers, and started looking through the sugar packs, in search of Sweet 'n Low, and put it in her cup.

"I think Equal is better," she said.

"But this is cheaper," I explained. She just nodded.

"So what brings you here, Marya?" I asked. "Just visiting your friend?"

"No," Shazia answered. "She actually went to Florida. Just thought she would stop by here and visit me as well since getting a visa is not that easy."

"Florida?" I asked this time facing Marya to make sure that she understood I was talking to her and not her friend. Not that I had anything against Shazia but it was Marya that I was trying to coax some words out of.

"Yeah, went to see U2," she finally answered. "I would have never gotten the visa but I begged the lady at the embassy to just let me go this one time. I swore that that is all I wanted. Besides, my

whole family is back in Pakistan. Luckily, she was a U2 fan as well and gave me a chance."

"Oh, I am big on U2 too," I said and I wasn't lying. She had gone to see them for their Popmart Tour, which had followed their latest album, Pop.

Granted the critics hadn't been too kind to their latest effort but to fans like us, anything Bono and the boys put out was worth it.

But when I look back at it, Pop isn't one of U2's best. A couple of songs are great but is that really enough? Sure. One is enough. My obsession on that CD was If God Will Send His Angels. Loved it. Had it on repeat in my CD Man.

CD Man?

I didn't mention that I was a big music buff without a decent system. All I had was this CD Man that I had bought from some guy at school for twenty bucks. He was upgrading to something fancier and wanted to get rid of his old one. So his old thing became my only thing. By the way, I did go all out on getting some new headphones after the old ones started to fade. Spent a dollar and change on getting a small new pair from a Seven Eleven.

Life was simple. And it was good.

"So how were they?" I asked.

"Awesome," replied Marya. "I was hoping that even if it's halfway decent, it will be worth all the shit I had to go through to get there. But it was way beyond what I thought it was going to be."

"I have never been to a concert. Any," I said. "I mean, when I hear these live versions of studio tracks, they just don't sound as good. And besides, there are all these crazy fans at the show, screaming and passing out."

"No, that is so stupid," Marya replied. "There are no people passing out. Unless its the heat or something. Screaming, yes. And the songs don't sound as good as the album versions because

they are not sitting in some fucking studio where they can do it over and over until they get it right."

"Okay, I will try to catch them the next time they come around."

I had three fries left on my plate when the girls got there. Now I had two.

So couldn't really offer them any. But I had been smoking pretty steadily.

"How many do you smoke?" Shazia asked as I lit another one.

"Just one," I replied.

"Bull," she said. "This is the third one since we got here and you were smoking at the Pub."

"I thought you meant at a time," I said. "Oh, I don't know. Its just that when people tell me each cigarette is another nail in the coffin, I tell them I have a multi-family house going."

They both laughed and I noticed that Marya had this almost childish way of laughing. A mix of giggles thrown in to make it the best looking laugh I had ever seen.

Chapter 12

"Beta," Taya ji said as I was heading towards the door.

"Yes, sir," I said. Maybe he had some more tips for me. Maybe he wanted to tell me a quicker way to get to the train station.

"Just don't freeze," is all he said as he laid back on the bed.

"I will try not to," I said as I headed out the door.

And, yes, I was a little confused. It was early September and there was a little chill in the air. But far from one that would make you freeze. We were in Rawalpindi, a kind of sister city to Islamabad, the country's capital. Winters did get cold but it never snowed. At least not around the cities. It snowed up in the mountains. Which made me think of my childhood days when my parents would get me in the car and we would head on up to Muree, one of the mountain towns, to see the snow. That was one of the recreations. Or you could go higher up the mountain to Nathia Gali or Ayubia. Just to see snow.

Something I had gotten sick of being in New Jersey. There you got snow delivered to your door and you stopped loving it once you had been out there with a shovel one too many times. Actually, snow was bearable up to eleventh grade, because then you got snow days. You got to stay home and watch the trucks cleaning up the streets outside, kids playing in the snow, and people slipping and falling. A person falling always seemed hilarious from a distance. I would laugh at first but then hope they were okay. Couldn't look away until they had gotten back up and walked a little further. Safely, I hoped.

But around twelfth grade, a little apprehension started creeping up on me.

I was going to move out of my uncle's place, go off to college and live in my own place. And I would need to get my own shovel for those times.

I was getting older.

I got on taya ji's Wespa and started it but couldn't get over what he had just said. It was chilly but how the heck could I or anyone freeze. It wasn't until Ghulam sahib brought me a letter from his son in London that I realized what taya ji had meant.

Chapter 14

No, you didn't flip too many pages. You were just on chapter 12, and now its 14. What happened to 13? I just wanted to skip over a chapter 13. Maybe I am superstitious. Or maybe I just choose not to push my luck. Its more of the later, even though there has to be some of the former to make the later happen.

That's it.

That is why there is no chapter 13.

So the girls and I were sitting at the diner talking.

As soon as I left the place, I fell. On the other hand, I realized that I was falling. It wasn't the alcohol. It was just the strangest feeling. Something that had been non-existent until a few moments ago. I brushed it off and headed home. But I had managed to make some plans with Marya since she was only staying for another week. Shazia was busy with her job and household stuff.

So I volunteered to take Marya around for shopping or whatever else she wanted. That is if she could trust me.

'Of course', was the response. For some reason this was not the first time that someone I had just met trusted me. But I was just that kind of person, honest to God. I never put up a facade. Never lied, cheated or attempted either one. That was the same reason Mr. Patel didn't hesitate in hiring me for his store. I also hate praising myself for something that was instilled in me by my parents and family. So then I should stop right now and move on with my tale.

❧

"Well, I have to go around and do some shopping. Everyone back in Pakistan will be expecting something," said Marya at the diner.

"Tell me when, and just give me a call at the store," I said.

"And then, of course, I have to buy some stuff for myself. Mostly cds," said Marya.

"I will just take you to store I go to for my music shopping," I said, not realizing that I had just lied.

"So is tomorrow okay? What time?" she asked.

"You tell me. I just have to let Patel know that I have to take some time off."

"Okay, I will give you a call then. But I do need a phone number," said Marya.

I gave it to her as we parted ways.

I had trouble sleeping that night. Just couldn't get over this new sensation that was overcoming my lonely existence.

And then it began.

Chapter 15

"So how was your first day, Beta Ji?" Taya Ji asked as I entered the house.

I was in terrible shape and the weather had nothing to do with it. It was actually pretty mild out.

"Okay," was all I managed to say.

"You don't seem okay? Hungry? I went and got some nans from Khan before. "And there is some leftovers from last night, if you don't mind food that's a day old," said taya ji.

"No, that is perfectly fine, sir."

Taya Ji always called me beta, which means son. The Ji was added on as an extra note of affection. Or you could add Jan. Jan means life and by addressing someone with that addition you were basically saying that the person was as dear as life. I never really got around to finding what Ji implied. But those were the common add ons. That is why I called taya ji, taya ji. Or I could do the same thing with my parents. Mom was ami and dad was abu. Unless I wanted something because then they would become ami ji or abu ji.

"Ghulam sahib came today," I said.

"Oh... And?"

"He had a letter from his son in London," I said.

"I should have explained that situation to you," Taya Ji said.

"Yes, that would have been very helpful," I said, this time a little angrily.

Taya Ji had taken me with him a few times to show me how things worked and to introduce me to the others that worked around there, like the guys who helped out the passengers with their luggage or kulis as they were called. And the guys working at the cafeteria at the station. And some of his regulars who would bring their letters to be read and their messages to be written. Ghulam sahib had been one of them.

I had met him on one of my introductory visits. His son had gone to London to get some kind of job that would pay better. He would send his parents money every month or whenever he could manage. He also had a wife and child who were living with his parents.

When Taya Ji had read his letter on that day I went with him, it was all about how his job was going well as a waiter in a Pakistani restaurant in London. And how he couldn't wait to get back to his loved ones in Pakistan.

"Because that letter had nothing to do with what you told Ghulam the other day," I went on.

"He was telling his father that he is very sorry for letting them down and marrying some girl over there. He doesn't want his father to let his wife and kid know. They won't understand that he did it to become a legal resident," I said my voice getting louder and angrier.

"It's the same thing he writes in every letter. I don't know how he is planning on handling it when he finally has to face them over here," Taya Ji said.

"Well, it would have been easier if you had told his father what was actually going on and not some fairy tale about how his son is doing so well over there," I said. "At least then his parents would have had some time to think over what's going on."

"Yes, but it would have broken Ghulam's heart. And then he would have to tell the son's wife," Taya Ji said.

"But it would have been better than whatever is going to happen now. The son is going to come back some day. He has to," I said.

"I know. I think about these things all the time," Taya Ji said. "But how did he react when you read him what was written?" Taya Ji asked.

"Well," I said a little sheepishly, "I didn't know what to do."

Taya Ji just stared back at me.

"So I lied," I said.

Chapter 16

I pulled along side the lawn and honked twice just like I told her I would. It took a couple of minutes but Marya came out of the house, said something to whoever was inside, closed the door and ran towards my car.

It was a little brisk outside, so she had a heavy shirt on. Must have been freezing for her since she wasn't used to this kind of weather being from Karachi which was like the Florida of Pakistan…hot, humid, and by the sea.

"Hello," I said as she got into the front seat.

"Hi," she replied. "So this is what you drive? Not bad," she lied.

It was an 1988 Honda Civic. Beige and banged up a little. Not by me, though.

That's the way I had bought it. The guy had been a little desperate for money and had let me have it for five hundred bucks. Besides, it had a hundred and thirty two thousand miles on it when I bought it a few months before in early '97.

"You are so full of it," I said. "At least give your lies a little effort," I (smiled?) said.

"No, really," she said. "Honda is pretty big back home."

"Yeah, but not in this shape," I said pulling onto the road. "Besides, I am a simple man. Even if I had a million bucks, I'd still drive something humble like this. As long as they get me to where I am going."

"That's a good way of doing things," she said.

I, of course, was smoking. I asked her if she smoked and if she wanted me to throw it out.

"No, but I did try it once. Got sick as hell, and never really tried it again," she said. "But you can smoke if you want, although you smoke a little too much."

"You see, you have to pick the right brand. These Parliaments are not harmful at all. I had to look around a lot before picking these. All these other cigarettes had the warnings that smoking cause lung cancer or emphysema or some other shit. But I picked these because they won't do me any damage," I said.

"Really? How so?" she asked.

"Because the warning on these says that smoking can cause birth defects. I don't have to worry since I am not pregnant," I said.

"Are you serious?" she asked.

"Of course," I said with an honest look. That was one of my talents.

I could look you straight in the eyes and tell you something that was the biggest lie you could come across. But I never lied. Just joked around because I would tell the person that what they had just been told wasn't the truth at all.

So then I smiled at Marya and said," I am just kidding, you know."

"Thank God, because I was starting to have second thoughts about you," she said.

"So that means that you actually had some initial thoughts about me which preceded these second thoughts," I said.

"Whatever," is all she said as I pulled onto the Garden State Parkway and headed south.

Chapter 17

"So how many are there?" I said looking at Taya Ji.

We were both sitting at Khan's Canteen on those scraps of wood, barely held together by some rope, that were known as stools in that establishment.

Taya Ji had his usual beige shalwar kameez on, with an Afghan cap thrown on to keep his head warm because it was a little chilly. Those Afghan caps, which had some kind of name I wasn't familiar with, were supposedly pretty warm. But I never liked wearing anything on my head. Even in the US, I had tried baseball caps and found them to be too congestive. Plus, I could never find one that would be so generic since I didn't really follow sports that much. Never did. Even when I was growing up in Pakistan, I didn't care about cricket, which was hugely popular, or any other sport.

As kids, my friends used to play around in the streets and never really had any loyalties to any sport in particular. One day we would feel like playing soccer, get some bricks to identify where the goal would be, and start playing soccer, or as we knew it, football. Other days, we would get a bat and tennis ball to play cricket. Many of the people living down our streets didn't like that too much because quite a few times we would hit the ball too hard and break somebody's window. But mostly I liked playing with a Frisbee.

That would be the extent of my sportsmanship. So when I came to the US, I wasn't too keen on sports either. And a double whammy turned out to be when I found out that field hockey was a female sport in the US. Back in Pakistan, it was the National Sport, played by "manly men".

But Taya Ji didn't answer my question. He took a sip of his tea and just looked out the road with the heavy traffic going by and the constant honking of the cars, motorcycles, buses, and rickshaws. You rarely heard anyone toot his or her horn in the US. In Pakistan though, the horn is used more often than the brakes.

"Who would believe that this was a third world country?" he said. "Look at all these cars. Everybody is in their cars."

He was right about that. There was a lot of traffic and it seemed to be getting worse. From the time I left in 1991 to the time I came back in '98, everything seemed to have quadrupled…the people, the cars, and everything else that comes with those two. Mostly men drove; the women generally didn't drive. The husband would hire drivers to take their wives, daughters, or mothers around.

Yes, Pakistan was an impoverished land.

"You didn't answer my question, sir," I said again. "How many have been believing the lies you have been telling them?"

He just stared out into the passing traffic and didn't say a word. I decided not to coax him any further. It wasn't any easy question I had asked. I was going to let it sink in and let him answer whenever he felt he could. He took a sip from his cup of tea and I just sat there nursing my bottle of Fanta. Some breakfast. But I had already had a toast with butter and orange marmalade. That would be enough to hold me off until lunch. Never was too big on tea. I had iced teas a few times when I was in the US. Then I got into the whole Long Island Ice Tea thing, and that was the end of my tea days.

"I don't know," he finally replied. "It just started happening. I thought it would be simple-read them their letters and write them if they wanted."

He went quiet again. There were a lot of laborers sitting at the Canteen. It was their launch pad before they went out to their jobs or went looking for work if they didn't have any.

"But it was not that simple. These people were bringing their hearts to me. How could I break them?" he went on.

"I used to consider myself a good Muslim. But how could I lie? It's a sin. But some of the truths I would have told these people would have been a greater sin in my eyes. The hell with the mullahs and what they are preaching. I had read somewhere that a lie that unites is better than a truth that separates. Not the type of thing that you will find in the Koran or be taught by your elders. But it seemed right to me."

"I know," is all I could manage to say.

"No, you don't know. How many letters have you read so far?" he said.

"Wait until Zeenat comes to you. Will you tell her that her husband is still looking for work in your America? That he spends his nights sleeping on some park bench because his landlord kicked him out? That he has no money to send her? That whatever he has sent her is money he got by begging people on the streets for some help? That he only eats once a day because that is about all he can afford after he sends her whatever few dollars he has made begging or working some menial job he managed to come by for a few days. You tell me what you would say to that woman who believes her husband is in the great America living the life Pakistanis dream about."

I didn't reply. I just lit another cigarette and looked out at the road and thought about all Taya Ji had said. And then I thought about Marya again.

It had been a few days since that had happened. Maybe she was fading from my memory. At least I wished it was so.

Chapter 18

I think I mentioned earlier that I never lied or cheated. Well, in case, if I didn't, let me say it now.

But 1997 is when it all changed. I started lying. But only because I had no idea what else to do. It just seemed like the right thing to do.

"How far is this store?" Marya asked.

"About half an hour," I replied.

"Really?" she said. "That seems kind of far. You mean there is no store that sells music close by?"

"Well, you did say that you wanted to go to the place where I went to get my shit. So I am taking you there," I said.

"Okay, whatever."

CD Turf was about five minutes away from where we were. But that would have been too quick. She was going back to Pakistan in a week and this was one of my last chances to spend some time with her... To get to know her better.

When I was growing up in Pakistan, my parents always encouraged me to read. At the time it seemed like they were pushing me to read. Many of my free days were spent getting dropped off at the British Council Library in Islamabad. Shortly thereafter the American Center opened on the same stretch of highway where my father's bank was located. Actually right across from the bank. So another place opened for me to be at when not in school.

They wanted me to go there and go through the magazines and newspapers. Time, Newsweek, and the likes, but initially I found the place boring. Then I stumbled onto a section where they had some books about movies, theater, and such topics. And I started loving the place. I was there to look at all the educational stuff. But I was going through the books that were all about Hollywood and the movies.

Why not? After all that was also part of America. I guess not many people bothered with that section because there would have been a lot of outrage if they saw some of the pictures in those books.

Pictures from movies like Last Tango in Paris. But all those books were in the journalistic vein. There were movie reviews from the New York Times and Washington Post. I had found a home.

I did look at other things, mind you, but they didn't have any books that were from authors that were interesting to me. They did have Nathaniel Hawthorne, William Faulkner, and Carson McCullers, but they didn't have Stephen King or anybody else that would have captured my interest. Just dry stuff. Although a work by Carson McCullers caught my eye. I didn't read it but just had the title stuck in my mind for the rest of my life. The Heart is a Lonely Hunter.

How true. How appropriate for that time I took Marya to CD Turf.

Was I a believer in that "love at first sight" theory?

No. Did that change the day I saw Marya?

No. It was not love at first sight at all. I think it was something that precedes the L word. Something almost as scary. Maybe even scarier. The urge to know this person better.

The urge to fall in love with a person.

Fucked-up is the only way to define it. I wanted to fall in love with her. Does that make sense? Because it didn't make any sense to me, which is why I took her to the CD Turf that was half an hour away. Maybe a little less than that, but I knew there was a CD Turf at Garden State Mall, nine or ten exits down the Parkway. So that is the way we were headed.

"By the way, how old are you?" I asked.

"Twenty-two," she replied.

"So you are older than me," I said, thinking that I may be starting to fall for an older woman.

"Really?" she said. "How old are you then?"

"Nineteen," I said.

"But you were at that pub. Don't you have to be twenty-one?"

"Well… I know people," I said smiling and taking a puff off of my cigarette.

Yes, I smoked while driving too.

"Okay, I guess," she said. And then she coughed a little cough. So cute.

"Is the smoke bothering you? Because it's killing me," I said.

She smiled and said," No, its okay."

"But honestly, if it is bothering you just tell me," I said.

"No, its fine. How far are we?" she said.

"Another ten minutes or so," I said. "You are not cold are you?"

Since I was smoking, I had the driver's side window cracked a little. I realized that I was being an awfully rude host. I threw out the rest of my cigarette and shut the window.

"Thank you," she said.

"No, I am sorry. I should know that it would be freezing for you Karachi folks," I said.

"Tell me about yourself."

"Like what?" she said. Then she just went on," Well I am an only child which may explain how I managed to talk my parents into letting me come here by myself. You know how impossible it is to be a female in Pakistan and do what I just did? Come to the US by myself and not for a cause that would be considered good over there. To go see a concert. And I did it. I guess my parents knew they could trust me. God knows I haven't done anything that would be even considered dishonorable back there."

❧

"Well, I did meet you in a bar," I said.

"Yeah, I guess that would be bad. But I swear it was just a one time thing. And I didn't want to stop there either. Shazia talked me into going," she said.

"Do you regret it?" I said.

"Actually," she said. And then after a brief pause, "no."

I didn't say anything in response. I actually wanted to but didn't know what to say. We had pulled into the mall parking lot and I pointed to the store where we were headed and just said, "see."

Then I started looking for a place to park and found myself distracted by something that seemed new to me. I liked this girl.

I actually liked her very, very much.

Chapter 19

"Are you going to be okay?" Taya Ji said as I headed to the door.

"Sure. Why wouldn't I?" I asked.

"No, no. Just wanted to make sure you can handle what you have gotten yourself into," he said.

"Taya Ji, it's not something to be proud of but I am pretty good at lying," I said.

"Okay but I don't like it when you call it lying. It's more than that.

You just reduce it to a common human trait," he said.

"Then what should I call it, sir?" I asked.

He thought for a few moments and then looked at me with a look that almost seemed like he was embarrassed.

"I guess it is lying," he said.

"Its all good, sir. Just not too sure about the ending," I said as I headed out the door.

क

It took about half an hour to get to the Rawalpindi Train Station. The weather was pretty mild for that time of the morning and traffic, surprisingly, wasn't too bad. One thing I should point out is that there is a lot of improvisation involved in the commute.

How so?

Well, there are laws and lights but there isn't anybody around to enforce them. People don't speed through a yellow light before it turns red… they speed through red lights. Nobody gives a damn. If you have a green light then you better slow down and make sure that people are stopped at the red, because odds are that they will just be coming along through the red as if its just an enlarged Christmas decoration hanging in the middle of the intersection. Or maybe it's because color blindness is rampant.

I don't know. There is no fear of getting pulled over, getting points on your license, and having your insurance go up.

People don't wait to get a license to drive. They just drive.

Actually, who am I to judge? I never got a license in Pakistan.

Just had my New Jersey Driver's License with me in case hell froze over and some cop pulled me over.

Didn't even know how that would happen. What would I do? Was the Wespa insured? Was there any registration or whatever?

I had no clue.

ಹ

I got to the train station, parked the scooter behind a fence where it would be visible to me and went to the table. I took off my little Eastpack backpack, which I had brought with me from the US and put it down on the ground next to the chair. I took a seat and then unzipped the bag to take my stuff out. A couple of ball point pens, a notepad, and an eraser. I had no idea why I had that last item since it was not going to work on the ink. But then I also had a bottle of Blanco or as it was called in the US, WhiteOut.

I was all set. Now just wanted someone to come along to let me save them.

ಹ

Good thing I had cigarettes. My Marlboro Lights from the US I had finished on the third day so now I was smoking Gold Leaf. It had taken some getting used to but was probably just as efficient at killing me as their American counterpart. I was on my third cigarette when an old lady hobbled up to me and sat down on the stool that was there for the clientele.

Yes, I was in business.

Chapter 20

"Where is Zain?" the old lady asked.

I guess she wasn't that old…in her sixties maybe. Back in the US, people in their seventies considered themselves young. God bless them, they stayed active and kept themselves busy. In Pakistan, they started considering themselves old as soon as they hit fifty.

"Actually, he won't be here anymore. I am his nephew, Irfan. I thought it was time for him to take it easy now. So I will try to take over," I said.

"Fine. But you don't look like you can read or write Urdu," she said.

"Don't worry, ma'am, I can do it just fine," I said hoping to stir some confidence in the woman.

Yes, I could do fine in Urdu. After all, I had stayed in the country until I was thirteen. Went to school, spoke the language, and never spoke English unless it was the only language being spoken when I was in the US. It kept me in touch with my origins, I believed. Speaking English was almost a status thing in Pakistan.

Parents would communicate with their kids in English in Pakistan so they would be prepared when they, hopefully, left that country to pursue a better future abroad.

My parents wanted me to speak English at home but I never did. It just felt odd. Why abandon something I had grown up speaking?

By the way, Urdu is pretty much like Hindi, the language predominantly spoken in India. Its written like Arabic, right to left, and spoken like Hindi. So you get a grasp of a couple of languages while knowing just one. Which is why I could talk with the Indian people in the US, without pushing them to try out their broken English. Subsequently, the language I took in high school had been Spanish. So there was that as another notch on my linguistic belt.

"Well, my name is Zakia, and you have to write a letter to my son," the old lady, now known to be as Zakia, said.

"Okay, just tell me what to do?"

"Tell him that I have found a very nice girl for him," she said.

"So its time for him to get married?" I asked.

"No, no. He is already married. But he just had his fourth child and it was another daughter. Four daughters," she said with a look that said something like her lack of faith in her bad fortune.

"So, what's the matter with that?" I asked knowing full well what was wrong in that woman's eyes.

"What is wrong?" she said, raising her voice. "I want a grandson. Not four girls to worry about. He is my only son and he has to give me at least one grandson.

The wife he is with can't do it," she went on. "I never liked her from the start but it was his father's friend's daughter, so we had to do it.

But now I have reason enough to have him leave her."

"And you don't have any daughters of your own?" I asked trying to reach some sort of sense with the woman.

"No," she replied as if I had asked the most moronic question which it was a little since she had told me it was her only son.

Only child made sense to me since it was hard to imagine that this old bag had gotten laid twice. Yes, that was very rude and judgmental of me, but by this point, I did not like her...for her outright disregard for her daughter-in-law and, maybe even, her son.

I guess it would be senseless to try to reason with her since her beliefs had been grounded in her mind long before I even entered the human race.

And I don't think she liked me... Just for the way I was... Wearing jeans ripped at the knees, a black t-shirt that said Nine Inch Nails and an earring in my left year. Only gay guys get their right ear pierced, I was told.

"So where is your son?" I asked.

"Lahore," she said as if I was supposed to know it.

Lahore, one of the oldest cities in the country and one whose name had bought me ridicule on quite a few occasions in the US.

"What is it? Some town full of prostitutes that was misspelled," they used to joke around.

La Whore. Yeah, very funny.

But memories aside, I had to write a letter I didn't want to. Taya Ji had told me to be cautious. Not to get offended or take anything personally.

So this is what he had meant.

Chapter 21

It was the oddest feeling. But it wasn't a new feeling - I had the same feeling many times before.

What made some folks back in the US call me a "pussy." Or some called me a "fag." What was it? I had done a lot of reading and come to know it as being referred to as empathy. Putting oneself in somebody else's shoes. To understand how and why they felt the way they did. At least that is how I saw it.

Or maybe I was a pussy or a fag. There had been kids in my class at Ridgewood High School who had been complete and utter assholes. But for some odd reason, I had ended up getting friendly with them. No, there were no ulterior motives. I just felt bad for them. I saw them as being lonely and misunderstood. I just felt that they didn't have any other way of letting it out.

And now I felt the same way about Zakia. Yes, that old lady who wanted her son to leave his wife because she kept on giving birth to daughters instead of sons. Yes, that old lady that I hated when we first met. That same old lady who had a mind set on things that I not only disagreed with but also hated. But for some odd reason, I felt bad for her. Poor Zakia, I thought. She thinks the way she does because that is all she knows. A product of her environment. Poor, uneducated, and in a rut that will never end. A mind frame that is blocking her from appreciating all she has been given in the form of her four granddaughters.

Poor Zakia who will always be craving something she has been molded to believe is the truth. Poor Zakia who will never understand what she has.

Poor Zakia.

Maybe I was a faggot-ass pussy.

So I was the sensitive type. The kind, according to magazines, that girls went for. A bunch of shit. Because I had seen it. The girls always went for the assholes who treated them like shit. I guess those magazines didn't have the balls to say it the way it was.

But I digress. That is easy to do when you are sitting there digging up shit that you thought was buried deep but have to face when you are trying to put yourself in perspective. After all, that is what makes you. At least, that is what made me. But there I go again... still digressing.

"Do your parents know?" Taya Ji asked.

"About?", I asked knowing full well what he was talking about.

"That you are back. That you are not in the US anymore. That you are barely half an hour away from them," he said.

"I don't know," I said. "Seriously, I don't have a clue."

But I knew that they didn't know. I would go to the pharmacy nearby, pay the guy ten rupees, and call up my parents from the quiet of the back room. Then I would talk to them and tell them that I was calling from the US and just wanted to let them know all was well. Good thing there weren't any Caller ID's around.

My father would have killed his only son if he knew the truth. Which is why I wasn't lying. I was just saving him from the aggravation.

"How would they just know unless you told them?" Taya Ji said.

"I don't know," I replied showing how unprepared I was for this kind of talk.

"Its getting late, I think I should head to the station now in case somebody is waiting," I said, knowing full well that nobody would be waiting.

"Okay then. Allah Hafiz," Taya Ji said.

"Khuda Hafiz," I said walking out the door. (The new thing was that you were supposed to say, Allah Hafiz, meaning that may Allah watch over you. That is what was supposed to distinguish good Muslims from the others.

Since I didn't consider myself a Muslim, I always said, Khuda Hafiz, meaning may God watch you. You see, I believed in God; just not the Muslim God. That is just how I was - stubborn in my beliefs. Raised as a Muslim but far from it for over a decade.

There were many reasons why Islam did not suit me. Reasons that I will touch on throughout my memories.

One, there always has to be a right way and a wrong way. Of all the religions and beliefs that are contaminating our planet, there has to be one that is right. Going about and finding it is a task that can take a lifetime. So what did I do? I just gave up. Surrendered.

Turned my back on what could have led to some tranquility. But what kind of eight year old stays up at nights and cries himself to sleep because of what his faith has taught him?

My best friend at my school in Islamabad was Amir. We were just inseparable growing up. I had known him since first grade. Our friendship led to a friendship between our parents since I would be over at his house a lot of times after school.

But then a realization struck me around the third grade. Amir's family was shia Muslim. Or shiites as they are known in the west.

His parents complied with all their Islamic duties.

They had even gone for the Haj, the fifth pillar of Islam that required all able Muslims to go to Mecca for the pilgrimage. But I was from a Sunni family.

And, of course, the Sunnis were right. Which meant that the shias were wrong.

And what happens with the wrong doers? They go to hell and face all kinds of horrors for eternity. And I didn't want my best friend to go to hell and burn for all eternity with his family. They were good people. I loved him like a brother. So I prayed and prayed for Allah to guide them, make them see the right path, and become Sunnis.

But that didn't happen. So I used to lie in bed at night and cry myself to sleep thinking about Amir's inevitable damnation.

The poor souls, him and his family, not knowing how wrong they were.

ॐ

I left the house, got onto the Wespa, and headed to the train station, all the while thinking how I was going to handle my lies today.

Chapter 22

Yes, that was me. The faggot-ass pussy.

I started off hating Ridgewood High School. It was all a bunch of white kids. On the other hand, there were a lot of Indians. They all hung out together.

So where was this Pakistani supposed to go?

Of all the classes, the most dreaded one was gym class. I didn't know shit about the sports they played. I think I mentioned already that I was never a sports-type guy.

But the most dreaded time of the day had to be lunch. Everyone had their own group in the cafeteria. Where the hell was I supposed to go? Thank God, they had the library. So that is where my lunch time was spent.

"Hey, dot head, do you spit or swallow?" came the question from a tall, white kid that I would later get to know as Chuck.

I just sat there at the table, went about going through my history book, and eating my chocolate Chipwich. And I also ignored the question that had just been asked.

"What are you fucking deaf, or you don't speak the language?" Chuck persisted as he stood there with his friends adoring this apparent stance he was taking against the new kid.

Yes, I was in the cafeteria. How and why? Well, the library was getting fumigated or something. So I had to come to lunch. I just saw an empty seat on one of the tables in the corner and took it.

The other kids at that table gave me an odd look and whispered something to each other but I just opened up the book bag, took out the World History textbook, and went about eating my Chipwich. That would serve as my lunch since I was going to eat when I got home.

“No,” I finally said to Chuck. “I am not deaf and I do speak the lingo. Just wasn’t sure you were talking to me.”

“Well, I was, Patel. And you didn’t answer my question. Do you spit or do you swallow?” he said, his followers giggling.

“First of all, I am not a Patel. Second, I don’t do either. Not like your mom, whose health shows that she must have gotten a lot of proteins from all that swallowing,” I said knowing full well that this was the do or die moment in my high school life.

I couldn’t back down because this would be my only chance at standing my ground. If I chickened out now, the rest of my high school days would be over because word would spread.

Surprisingly, Chuck didn’t hurl anything in my direction. Just muttered,” mother-fucking nigger” under his breath, turned around and walked away with his followers, who weren’t that enthusiastic any longer.

“By the way,” I said as he was walking away, “I prefer to be called a sand nigger.”

Yes, I had set my foot down against the biggest bully in the cafeteria.

That’s when I first got to know Mike. He was a skinny, white kid who happened to be sitting at the table I had chosen.

“You got balls, man,” he said grinning.

“Two actually,” I said knowing that it wouldn’t be too hard to survive now that I had stood up to someone while sitting on my ass and not losing my demeanor.

Yes, life was getting to be better.

Chapter 23

The air was a little chilly but I still had my same stuff on. Blue jeans, a black t-shirt, and a flannel shirt over it. Unbuttoned, of course.

"Why do you always wear a shirt? It's not going to keep you warm since its always unbuttoned," my aunt had asked me numerous times when I was in the US.

"Pockets," was my response. "So I can put my things away without losing them."

"Oh yes, your cigarettes and lighter. Right?" she said.

"Pretty much."

I had never hidden my smoking from anyone. If it was going to be my new thing, then I made sure everybody knew I did it. Never hide who you are, is what I believed.

Why didn't I quit, they started asking after a while, because they had figured I would give it up after trying it out for a while. Was I addicted that badly? I used to tell that it wasn't really an addiction. More of a hobby.

'Whatever', they would say. 'You will regret it one day.' How do I explain that I regretted it even before I started it.

Nobody would understand. Nobody could understand.

When I got to the train station, it wasn't as busy as it usually was.

Maybe because I was a little early. It was only eight in the morning. Taya Ji was still in bed when I had left. He probably had woken up when I started the Wespa. This made me realize that if I was to ever leave this early again, I should take it a little further away from the house and then start it.

People at the train station knew who I was by now. There were the usual greetings from the kulis, or porters, and others who worked there. There were people getting ready for the morning crowd at the cafeteria. The station manager was making his rounds and acting like he was in charge. Which he was, but you have to remember that it was Pakistan. Just because your title was boss, didn't mean you were the boss.

For some reason, after the hellos, it seemed that they would talk in lower voices with each other. Obviously, it would have to be something about me since I was the only one within earshot. But I never let things like that bother me.

I sat down at my table, took out an old Stephen King paperback, Misery, put on my headphones, and started listening to my CD Man.

But, of course, I had to light a cigarette. Now I was smoking Gold Leaf, a cigarette that I had picked, once my US stash had run out.

I was hoping that not too many people would show up today. I just wasn't in the mood.

But until someone did, I had to put up with the toughest of company... myself and my head full of ghosts.

Who would I think about today? Obviously, whomever I didn't want to think of, would be the guest of honor. That is just how things worked.

Chapter 24

"Dude?", Matt said turning around and back really quick.

"Yeah?", I said looking up from the test in front of me.

We were sitting in Mr. Martin's world history class. I had no idea what the answer to the question was so I marked B. Kids had said that if you ever have to guess, always pick C.

I, of course, had to be different. So I always picked B.

"Is it true?", Matt asked keeping an eye on the door since Mr. Martin, the trusting fellow that he was, had stepped out of the room for some reason or other.

I looked at the sheet. There were no true or false questions there.

So what the hell was Matt talking about?

"What?", I asked.

"That Muslims can have three wives at the same time?", he asked.

Of course, I should have known that I wasn't safe from that question.

Nobody had asked me that at Ridgewood High yet. It was inevitable that somebody would. They all knew that I was from a Muslim family. The only one in this town, ruled by Catholics and over run by Hindus. No, I didn't have anything against either one but there were really a lot of Indians in that town. I was surprised that the mayor was a white guy.

"Kinda," I replied.

"What the fuck do you mean, kinda? That is awesome," Matt said. "I'd go for Linda, Jen, and Kelly. That would be awesome. A different one every night or all three at the same time. Maybe two."

"Your fat ass would be lucky if you landed even one," I thought to myself.

I would never say anything like that because, no matter, how rude or crude a person may have been, I just couldn't bring myself to hurt them; with words or otherwise.

That would be stooping to their level.

"It's not that simple," I said.

"Simple? You have three bitches at your hand all the time. Where's the complication?" he said.

"I will explain later. Gotta finish this test," I said.

"Fine," he said. "I don't even bother. We are just in ninth grade. Eleventh and twelfth are when you should start worrying because that is all that the colleges will look at. They don't give a shit about how you did in ninth."

"I know," I said. "But what the fuck, I figure."

"Okay go back to your test. Then after class you gotta tell me how to become a Muslim."

And then there was something else to look forward to.

ॐ

"Beta, are you sleeping?" the tired sounding voice asked.

I moved my hand away from my face really quickly and replied," No, no. Just relaxing since it was so quiet."

It was Sheikh Sahib standing in front of me with a couple of envelopes in his hand.

And I really wasn't sleeping. Nobody had come to me all morning and all I had been doing was smoking. After five or six cigarettes I had decided to lean back in my chair, close my eyes, and see what happened. What had happened was just memories – memories of my days at Ridgewood High and Josh's Pub. I was surprised I hadn't thought too much of… her.

Maybe she was fading. Or I wished it was so.

"I have these for you to read and then a couple of things you can write for me," Sheikh Sahib said.

"Sure, whatever you need, sir," I said.

He was an elderly man, around sixty or so, with white hair and a white beard. He looked a little odd at the time since he was dressed in a dark beige shalwar kameez with open sandals on his feet. Bata, the sandals said on the side. I was surprised since you didn't come across Bata that much anymore.

I figured they had gone out of business since everyone in Pakistan also wanted Nike or Reebok. But a lot of stuff that ended up on feet there was probably from Bata with a Nike or Reebok sticker slapped on to hike up the prices.

"What do you have, sir?" I asked.

"Well this looks like a bill from the water company. I don't understand how they have the courage to charge us for the filth that comes out of our faucets. My wife always wants to boil the water before we use it for drinking for cooking or anything like that. I ask her why? We have grown up this far drinking that stuff. I don't even go to the doctor."

"Maybe there is some secret healing power in that filth," he said, sarcastically .

"Yes, sir," I said opening one of the envelopes. "This is your water bill for the past month."

"I will just go to their office and pay it," he said. "I just brought it along since the mail just came and it was with this other envelope which you have to read. I think it's from my son."

I looked at the envelope and saw the stamps on it. They were from the UAE, or United Arab Emirates. That is where Dubai was and that is where his son was living.

"Yes, sir," I said," it looks like its from your son. How would you like me to read it?"

That is where things got a little tricky. Some people wanted me to read to them word for word. It gave them a sense that they were listening to their loved ones. Others, like Sheikh Sahib, just wanted me to read the thing and give them the gist of it.

What was the point of this letter? What did their son or daughter want or need? Or what news had they? Was it good or bad?

"Just tell me what he says," he said. "You can leave out all his junk about how much he misses us or whatever. Just tell me what he wants now."

Yes, the distance had surely made the father and son closer.

Chapter 25

"Hello?" a male voice answered.

"Oh, hi," I said. "Can I please speak to Marya?"

"She's not here," the guy replied sounding indifferent as if he was being forced to carry on this conversation.

"When will she be back?" I asked.

"I don't know. She went back to Pakistan as far as I know, so who knows when she is coming back. Maybe next time Bono and his boys are here," he said.

My heart sank as I replied with an angrier tone," its *Bono*," since he had said it like he was pronouncing Sonny Bono's last name.

"Yeah, whatever," he said. "Can I help you with anything else or is that it?"

"No, thank you," I said. And then giving it a second thought, "how about Shazia?"

"Yeah, she's here," he said and then yelled out "Shazi," away from the phone.

I waited a few moments and then a feminine voice answered, "Hello?"

"Hi, Shazia. This is Irfan… remember me?" I asked.

"Oh, yes, how are you?" she said.

"I am okay. Did Marya leave?" I asked, trying not to sound too desperate.

"Yes, she managed to get a seat on that PIA flight," Shazia said.

ॐ

Now for a little explanation about what just happened. The guy who answered the phone was probably Bilal, Shazia's husband. He had one of those Pakistani names that I had figured I could have used when moving to the US. It would be easier for the people here to come up with a Nickname. Bilal could be Bill. Or another such name was Jameel which could become Jimmy or something. However, there was no easy way about Irfan. People had tried to give me a name that would be easier for them but I had left it up to them.

"Do you have a nickname?" I was asked numerous times.

"Nope, but if you want to give me one that is easier for your primitive tongues to pronounce, go ahead," I always said.

They never tried. Everybody ended up learning Irfan. Though there were people, whom I had known since I first came to the US who continued to mispronounce it. Whatever. I didn't care as long as I knew that it was me they were addressing.

A lot of friends just called me Irf, but they said it like it was Urf. Like I said, whatever.

ॐ

"So she got that flight," I said.

"Yeah, somebody cancelled so she got their seat since she was on the waiting list," Shazia said.

I could help thinking... Why did she want to leave so soon? What was her hurry? It was almost as if she was trying to runaway or something. Marya had flown in on PIA, Pakistan International Airlines. Her return ticket had been open so she would have had to go to the airport and wait to see if there were any seats available.

Unfortunately, for me, there had been a seat available. How I had hoped to God that she wouldn't get the seat and be forced to stay a little longer. Long enough for me to tell her what I should have done when I dropped her off after our stop at CD Turf and a couple of other stores that day.

But she was gone.

My heart just sank. I kept the phone in my hand as I stood there trying to figure out what exactly was going on. I just leaned against the wall and then slowly slipped down, squatting on the floor. Then I just sat there with my back leaning against the wall, the phone in my hand and no clue as to what was unfolding. Inside me or outside me. No clue. I didn't tell her. Anything. Everything.

Then I did something I never did inside.

I took out my pack of cigarettes and pulled one out of the pack. I gave it a look thinking if I wanted to do it. Then I pulled out my lighter, lit it and started puffing while squatted on the floor.

My hand became my ashtray as I put the phone down on the floor next to me.

And then the phone rang. I looked at it after the first ring, thought about answering it, and realized that it couldn't be her. So I just let it ring since nobody else's phone call mattered at that time.

Fuck it, I thought as the answering machine went on after the third ring and I heard some stranger's voice talking about the very important nature of the phone call regarding my Citi Bank Visa card.

Then the loud siren started sounding as I realized I had totally ignored the smoke alarm in the hallway.

Shit, I thought as I struggled to get off the floor and thought about what to do, hoping the neighbors had not called the fire department.

Then I realized that I still couldn't believe she had left.

Maybe the plane never took off because there were engine problems. Maybe the pilot got a phone call telling him to stay put since his wife had gone into labor and was having their baby.

Maybe this… or maybe that.

I just couldn't believe she was gone.

Chapter 26

"Hello?" said a female voice that I immediately recognized as belonging to my mother.

"Hello. Guess who?" I said.

"Irfan," the excitement was obvious as she replied. "Beta, how are you? Where are you?

You haven't called in months."

"Well, I am still here in New Jersey," I lied. The lying was starting to get easier and easier.

I didn't like that. But once again, it was only to shield the poor lady's heart from breaking.

Her only son, sent to get a good education, a better future, and fulfill her dreams.

Turned into a failure, a dropout, and back where he had started. Of course, I didn't tell her the last part. I had gone to the pharmacy or chemist as they were called there, given him ten rupees to make a phone call. It wasn't enough according to him and I had ended up giving him another ten. All for a phone call that was going to take a few minutes and go no further than ten or fifteen miles.

"How do you like college?" she said. "Your father just went out to get some things from the market."

She always did that. Asked one question and immediately followed it with some observation that had nothing to do with the question and cut off the other person's answer. But I hadn't answered her. So she had just interrupted my silence.

"Its okay," I lied some more.

"You didn't make some girlfriend there did you?" she asked. "I told you that if you do something like that, she has to be a Muslim. Or at least become a Muslim if she wants to be my daughter in law. But I did always want you to marry a Pakistani girl."

She darn knew that I wasn't religious. She had actually taken it pretty hard when I told her that I couldn't keep calling myself a Muslim since I didn't agree with the religion. I had told her that when I had come back to Pakistan for a visit during high school. And she had blamed my father for it all... for sending me to the US. For thinking that it would give me a better future. A better future?

Without Allah and Mohammed, there was no future. She actually didn't talk to me during that visit until I was leaving. Then she had kissed me with tears in her eyes and told me to think about it real hard.

She gave me an English translation of the Koran to take with me. Maybe English could shed some light into my darkened mind.

It suddenly hit me that I couldn't talk for much longer. I had to tell her the truth.

"Ami," I said, "I left school."

"What?" she said in a voice that made me rethink my timing of this revelation.

"I just didn't want to do it anymore. It just was getting so repetitive. I have been going to school since I was four. There's no end in sight. I wanted to rest," I said realizing that all that was coming out of my mouth was such gibberish. Excuses.

"But you were doing so good," she said.

"Yes, but I didn't like it. I didn't have any heart for it. Just did it because you and abu wanted me to. Not because I wanted to."

"So what do you want to do?" she said. "Do that but get an education first. Then do what your heart pleases."

I was quiet.

"I just need some time, ami. To figure out where I want to go and what I want to do," I said.

"Beta, do what you think is right. After all, we just want the best for you. That is all your abu and I have tried to do for you," she said.

"Fine take some time off but don't stay away from your education for too long."

"I will try, ami," I said. "But I have to go now. Give my salaam to abu."

"What should I tell him?" she said.

"I don't know. Tell him the truth," I said.

"I will see. Allah Hafiz," she said.

"Khuda Hafiz," I said putting the phone down. That was enough for the poor woman. No need to tell her that I was actually back in Pakistan, living with taya ji, sleeping on the floor, and eating from some place that would be a long way from what they had fed me while growing up.

Yes, things were going somewhere. No idea where, but somewhere.

As my mother and I ended our talk, she said Allah Hafiz while I replied with a Khuda Hafiz.

Just another sign of my stubbornness. Growing up as Muslim kids, we were always taught to say *Khuda Hafiz* when saying farewell. What it means is that may God watch over you.

Then a little while ago, it all changed.

Muslims started saying *Allah Hafiz*, meaning that may Allah watch over you.

That was their way of distinguishing themselves from others. The Muslim God was Allah, while Khuda just meant God. I refused to change. Even when I talked to people while I was in the US, I just said that I was from a Muslim family. Didn't mean that I was a Muslim. In Pakistan, I had grown up going to a madrasa, or religious school, after my usual school. We read the Koran, we learned about the history, and basically learned how to be good Muslims so we could go to heaven after we died. I ran to the mosque whenever we could to say our prayers, which were five times a day.

Around fourteen years of age, while I was in the US, I started thinking about the way I was raised as a Muslim. I started doing what was forbidden. I started asking questions. Why did we have to read the Koran in Arabic? Why couldn't we just read it in whatever language we spoke? This way, at least we could understand it. But no, all good

Muslims were supposed to learn Arabic and read it in Arabic, the way it was intended. That made sense since I do believe things lose their meaning in translation. Okay, but why did we have to pray five times a day to thank Allah for everything? But shouldn't we thank the Lord because we want to and not because He demands that from us? If I did somebody a favor, I would tell them to thank me. If they thanked me then fine. If they didn't, then that won't stop me from ignoring them in their time of need the next time.

That is how I was. And the call to prayer, five times a day, began with "Allah Akbar," meaning Allah is great. That started striking me as something too human, i.e. to praise yourself. For me, modesty was a trait more divine. But, once again, that was just me.

And then there was the promise of rewards for leading a good life that made me finally abandon the religion. In heaven, men were promised so many beautiful virgins if they had led a good Islamic life. Most of my American friends used to laugh about how they would stick to this creed for rewards like that. But that was what did it for me.

If I was fortunate enough to find my true love, she would be the only one for me. Even in the so called afterlife, I would want to be with her. Not with a harem full of beautiful virgins. And that is what ended my affiliation with Islam as a follower. I couldn't follow something I found so many flaws in. It was not divine - it just wasn't.

God help me, but I just couldn't live the lie in hopes for a better after life. Besides, I would kid around that in the afterlife, I would probably know a lot more people down in hell than I would in heaven.

So those were my theological leanings.

Chapter 27

"What happened to baba ji?" she said hesitatingly as she walked up to the table.

I, of course, was sitting there smoking. I did have my CD Man playing some Limp Bizkit. Surprisingly, Break Stuff had just ended, and there was that brief period of silence when she had asked her question. Good timing, is all I could think.

"Oh, he is retiring. Not voluntarily. But I am making him," I said, pulling out the small ear pieces I had bought from a 7-11 back in the US; heck, a dollar and change wasn't a bad price.

"Oh," is all she said as she started to turn away. Maybe I wasn't really presenting myself that well to these people. As if my clothing weren't enough to cause stares but I had to sit there with my CD player at a volume that could be heard by anyone near me. And, on top of that, the music didn't sound too appealing.

"But I can help you," I said. She stopped, turned back around, and gave me another look.

I put the CD player down and put my cigarette out on the ground.

"Uhh, I had this letter," she said pulling a letter out of her purse and handing it to me. Her hands were almost ready to shake. You know, that stiffness that takes over when you are thinking about whether or not you should complete what you have already started.

I reached over and took it from her.

"Have a seat," I said pointing to the chair across from me.

She sat down and did so like she had done pretty much everything since walking up to my table. Hesitatingly. Giving it a lot of thought as if she was thinking why she hadn't walked away when she saw a stranger where she was expecting a familiar face.

She must have been around twenty or so. Probably up to my chin if we were standing face to face. Dark hair that was tied together with a rubber band behind her back. She had very light skin which made me think that she was probably a *pathan*. Those were the people from one of the northern provinces of Pakistan, a.k.a. the NWFP - North West Frontier Post. Those people could easily pass for Caucasians. Did I mention that she had these gorgeous hazel eyes?

Well, she did. And she was absolutely beautiful.

"My name is Irfan," I said opening the letter.

"My name is Marya," she said. Still a little hesitant but not as hesitant as my hands became while opening the letter and hearing her name.

I absolutely lost it at that moment. But I think I mentioned before that I am an absolute stoic.

I can tell the biggest lie with the straightest face... one of my secret talents. One of my only talents, probably. So I lost it when she told me her name was Marya. But I lost it on the inside.

"Well, Marya, what can I do for you?" I said.

She started going through her battered looking pocket book, or purse, as they were generally referred to in Pakistan. Then she pulled out a letter that seemed like it had been around the world before it got to her, and slowly put it down on the table, still not sure if I could be trusted.

Now I did mention that I lost it. Why? Because I just couldn't get over the fact that her name was Marya.

I mean, this horny as heck nation with the population growing out of control, and a shortage of names. Didn't parents have any other names besides the ones they kept slapping onto their babies.

Marya.

Alanis Morrisette probably wouldn't recognize this as being ironic because to her it would be all about having *too many spoons when all you need is a fucking knife*. This wouldn't be ironic. Maybe just strange.

Maybe she should have consulted me before putting out her record. But it wouldn't have sold shit if I had been involved.

I took the letter from Marya's hand and looked it over before opening it.

It was from England with a stamp profiling the Queen's head. Yeah, I thought since I recalled some British stamps I had back in my stamp collecting days. I could probably make a nice chunk of money if I found one of the British stamps I had with a picture of the happily married Prince Charles and Diana on it.

"And who is this from?" I asked nearing my opening of the letter.

"My husband," she said putting a damper on my mood. Why? Because I was starting to like her. I had no idea about her personal life or anything so it can be said that it was purely physical. And did I mention that she was beautiful. Dark hair, light skin, and a pair of very shy hazel eyes.

"He's in England?" I said realizing what a stupid question since I was opening a letter, from England, which she had informed me was from her husband.

Chapter 28

"Hello?" a voice I immediately recognized as belonging to Shazia said.

"Hi," I said," this is Irfan."

"Oh, how are you?" she said. I knew she wasn't expecting me to call since she had already told me that my object of interest, Marya, had left.

"I am okay," I said. Since it was a phone conversation and she couldn't see me, I rolled my eyes and probably made a face that said, "let's get this shit over with."

I hated the petty bullshit that was just filler for a lack of material to carry on a conversation.

I hated it in real life and I hated it more at this moment since I really didn't give a crap about how she was doing. Yes, that was not very nice of me. But, like I always justified it for myself, it was all good if nobody knew. Remember, a lie told for a good reason?

Well, this was one of those many occasions and I just hoped she wouldn't go into any details.

"So how can I be of assistance?" she said after a brief pause.

It took a little effort but I managed to get it out.

"I was wondering if you could give me Marya's phone number in Pakistan?" I said. Then I added, "Or if there's any other way of contacting her. Email address or something like that."

After I had added on that last part, I realized that my inquiries were reeking of desperation.

"Well, she doesn't have a phone number of her own, since its lucky if you can get even a single line in Pakistan," said Shazia. "I do have her number but its probably going to be answered by her mother."

That could be a little tough. Parents wouldn't take too kindly to a guy calling their daughter. Pakistan was like that. Daughters were given extra supervision. My hope lay in the fact that these parents were liberal enough to not care too much about this kind of thing. After all, they had let their daughter go to the US, by herself and to see a music concert.

"That's okay," I said. "I am sure that I am not the only guy who has ever called her."

"Yes," said Shazia, "but the thing is..."

"What?" I asked after that brief hesitation sounded never ending.

"Well, she is engaged," said Shazia.

"Oh, so she has a fiancée," I said realizing how stupid and pathetic I sounded with that observation.

She was engaged so, of course, she had a fucking fiancée.

"She didn't mention anything about that," I said.

"Yeah, well, you know," said Shazia.

No, I did not know. If I knew, I would not have asked this stupid bitch.

ꕥ

This was getting bad since my mind was becoming something I never wanted it to become; bitter and spiteful.

"Okay, bye, then," I said hanging up.

My life was becoming a soap opera. At least it was starting to have those twists and turns that desperate writers, trying to move a plot moving, came up with. Life was getting interesting. Not for me, though.

Chapter 29

I think it is time for me to do something I haven't done in a while. It is time for me to digress. I am not sure what I should turn to for digression, but profanity sounds like a good idea.

I don't use profanity. Yeah right, you are probably thinking, since I have dropped the "F" bomb quite a few times already. Okay, so I am not entirely correct in claiming that I don't use profanity. But, here's the trick.

Verbally, I rarely use profanity. Well, it depends on the company I am in… I have never used profanity in the presence of those who are older than I am. (Okay, maybe I have done that a few times but it was needed. Seriously. And I had made sure that these elders were using such language before I got into it. .)

In Pakistan, we kids never had the courage to utter any foul language in front of those who were older than us, regardless of the fact that they were using this kind of language in front of us. That is just the way things were. A little respect. No, it had nothing to do with song by Erasure. Like I said, that is just the way things were. If someone caught you using such language they wouldn't refrain from giving you a little beating. And it didn't have to be your parents. Anybody, and I mean anybody, who was older than you and heard you use that kind of language, would give you a spanking. If it wasn't your parent, they would give you a spanking and then pull you by the ear and take you in front of your parents. Then they would inform the parents about what they had heard you say. They would leave and it would be your parent's turn to give you a few hits. No, there was no such thing as child welfare people who would question this disciplining as being child abuse. That is why, according to the elders, kids were so much better in Pakistan than those spoiled and rotten ones in other nations.

You didn't curse. Actually, you didn't even hint at having prowess of any vulgar language.

And that was one of my culture shocks upon my fresh arrival in the USA.

Everybody cursed. Kids, grown ups, students, teachers… everyone. Not in front of each other sometimes but there were always slip ups.

"Do you even know what *fuck* means?" I asked a bullying kid at one time.

He must have been around ten or eleven and had been very liberal with the word in front of his friends at the Patel's store while I was working there.

Sure, he had said and gone into the significance of what the word had started to meant.

"Actually," I had said," it is an abbreviation, or acronym. Fornication Under Carnal Knowledge," I went on.

"When people were caught committing adultery in old days, they were put into those wooden things with their hands and legs pinned down. I forget what they were called. But they would be put in public squares with the letters FUCK imprinted on those things to let passer bys know the reason for their punishment. Kind of like a public humiliation thing. So that is where the word "fuck" came from. Kind of lost its purpose over the ages.

So I would give those kids a little history lesson in the midst of my lecturing. Discouraged them from using such language by attaching a history lesson to their frequent vocabulary. Was I right about my history? I think so. I was pretty sure I had heard it somewhere. But that was the gist of a lot of my knowledge. Heard it from people I would come across. I tried not to question a lot of it. Just picked them apart. Things I liked were put into the "truths" file in my head. Those I didn't like, were discarded and hopefully forgotten. Didn't always work out in the later case.

And that I think is enough of a digression. Now back to life.

Chapter 30

"What is a good card for Pakistan?" I asked.

"I don't know," the guy behind the counter replied. "Do I look like I call Pakistan?"

He continued, "we have those charts over there. You can look and see what's good."

Yes, the guy wasn't very pleasant to deal with but having worked at the Patel's store, I realized that I deserved that kind of answer for asking such a question. I was asked those kinds of questions at the store all the time and had to put up with the people who asked them. If I knew them, I would give them a smart-ass response.

But those responses were only given knowing that the person knew I was kidding around. That I wasn't serious. But this guy gave no such indication. He just wasn't very pleasant. So I went over to the charts and looked for a good rate for Pakistan.

"I will take an Instant Blue for five dollars," I said coming back to the counter. "It says it will give me thirty-two minutes."

He didn't give a damn how much time it would give me. For all he cared, it could give me thirty- two seconds. He just turned around, took down a card and put it on the counter. I paid him, thanked him, and walked out of the store.

Then the search began for a phone booth. There were plenty along the road but I needed one that would give me a little privacy. There were people walking around and I didn't want anyone I knew noticing me at a phone booth.

I picked one around the corner from Kenmar Bakery. A little darkened corner but perfect for me. I had passed it countless times but never given it a second thought. I pulled out my wallet, took out the phone number Shazia had given me, and picked up the phone. Thank God, there was a dial tone.

I flipped over the card and saw that I needed a coin to scratch off the pin number. I never carried change but I did have my fingernails that I used to scratch off the number. I went through the process. Dial the access number, pick English as my language of choice, enter pin number, and then the destination number.

The female voice said that I had twenty-one minutes for the call even though the chart had said thirty-two. But I didn't really care. After a brief pause, the bell rang at the other end of the world. I stood there and hoped that the phone would be answered by Marya since I didn't have much time and really wouldn't know what to say if somebody else answered. One ring. Two rings. Three rings. Each one seemed to be an hour apart. On the fourth ring, somebody picked up.

"Hello?" she said.

It had been a while but I knew that voice.

I had been waiting for this moment and when it came, I didn't do anything. I couldn't do anything. I just didn't know what to do. So I hung up. As I was doing so, I could hear another hello. I almost pulled the phone back to my ear but decided instead to go ahead with what I was doing.

I hung up. I looked around to see if anybody was around. Nobody. Besides, it was dark and cold. Around ten o'clock at night. The ten-hour time difference meant it was eight in the morning in Pakistan. She was probably just waking up. Or I woke her up. Whatever.

I just sat down on the sidewalk by the phone, leaned against the wall, and lit a cigarette. I tried not to think too much but that is all I could do. Think about her. Why had I tried to call her? What was I expecting? I knew that she was engaged. I knew she was getting married.

But it was probably an arranged marriage. Some guy that her parents had picked... Some guy she had nothing in common with... Some guy she was being forced to marry.

Maybe I still had a chance.

I put out the cigarette on the sidewalk and threw it into the planter next to me. Then I got back up and picked up the phone again.

I went through the ritual I had just completed not too long ago. Dial the access number. Enter the pin number. But the voice this time said I had two dollars and sixty five cents remaining. How? I hadn't said a single word. Then I realized that it was probably the stupid connection charges. That's how those calling cards got you. Upon entering the destination number, it turned out I only had eleven minutes left.

That would be enough. I hoped to God it would be enough.

ॐ

The bell rang. Then it rang again. This time she didn't pick up until the fifth ring.

"Hello?" she said, this time sounding a little agitated. Who could blame her? It was early in the morning and she had probably just woken up.

"Hello," I managed to say it this time.

"Who is this?" she asked.

"Irfan," I said.

"Who?" she asked.

"Irfan. Remember me. From Josh's Pub in New Jersey. You and your friend stopped in there," I said.

A little quiet and then, "Oh, how are you? I never expected you," she said. "Did you just call a few minutes ago?"

"Yes. But it got disconnected for some reason. I am using some calling card so have to put up with that shit," I said.

"Anyway, how are you?" she asked again.

"I am okay. I hope I didn't wake you," I said.

"Oh, I was up already. Don't worry," she said.

What the hell was I talking about? Such petty bullshit. And time was running out on the card. It would probably disconnect at any moment. I tried to come up with something that could clear the way for what I was trying to say.

"I called up Shazia and got your number. It took a little effort but she gave up eventually," I said.

"Oh, she's like that," Marya said.

Should I go ahead and just say it? I had no idea what to do.

"Yeah, well I was thinking about you and wanted to talk to you," I managed to finally say.

"What's on your mind?" she said.

Okay, I had to do it.

"Well, I have been thinking about you a lot. I am sorry," I said.

She was quiet for a moment and then said, "Why are you sorry?"

"It's just that," I started to say, "I really liked the time we spent together. I could really talk to you. I just liked being around you." And now to say it. "Marya, I think I am in love with you. I am sorry. I just couldn't help it. Hang up any time you want. I just had to say it."

There was absolute silence. Maybe she was thinking of what to say. Of letting me down easy.

"Hello?" I said.

Nothing. Dead silence. Then I realized the card had finished. I just stood there. Then I put the receiver back in its place, sat down on the sidewalk, and lit another cigarette.

"Shit," I said aloud and then leaned my head against the cold brick wall behind me.

What the hell was I thinking when I just bought one calling card? It was only five dollars.

I should have bought at least two and the store was probably closed by now. Or it would be by the time I got there. Shit, shit, shit. That was all I could think as I sat there on the sidewalk smoking one cigarette after another.

"Hey, what the hell are you doing?" A voice that seemed a little familiar broke my solitude of misery.

Then a bright glare lit my face. Somebody was shining a flashlight in my face.

"Irfan," Ken said walking towards me. "What the fuck are you doing sitting there like that?"

It was Ken Grafton or Kenny as I usually called him. One of the young cops on KPD, Kinsville Police Department.

I knew him from stopping in the grocery store where I worked. Plus he had ended up being one of my drinking buddies at Josh's Pub. A lot of cops hung out there after work and he was one of them. One of the younger ones, around twenty-five or so. Which is why he usually got handed a flashlight and had to walk up and down the streets at night before he could go in and rest behind the desk until morning. All the cops worked 7 to 7. From 7 am to 7 pm. Or the other way around.

I guess he had started at 7 pm and would be there till the am.

"Nah, I just paged someone," I lied. "I am just waiting for him to call back."

"Dude, it's freezing out here," he said. "Don't you have a phone at home? Or are you just coming from JP?"

"No," I said, "I was there earlier today. Around 8 or so. It was pretty dead so I decided to go home. Just had to call up Steve about something. So I paged him and the asshole hasn't called back yet. I think I will just leave. It's been almost fifteen minutes already," I said as I started to get up.

"Yeah, go home, dude," Ken said turning around and flashing his light up and down the sidewalk.

"Alright. I will see you around then," I said as I walked towards my car.

"Good night," Ken said walking away.

"Good night," I replied as I started to drift back to what I had just done.

I was probably going to scare the girl by telling her I was in love with her. Was it too soon?

Was there anything that was supposed to precede that? I had no idea. It wasn't like I was a pro at this sort of stuff.

I had never even had a girlfriend during high school. Friends who were girls, but not a "girlfriend."

Shit, I thought as I started the car and started fumbling with the radio.

Chapter 31

"What's up, Pan?" Jim said walking into the store.

It was the quiet time of the day and I was just sitting behind the counter reading The Daily News.

"Not much, sir," I said looking up from the paper.

"God damn it. How many times do I have to tell you not to call me sir," Jim said. "Makes me feel old. Call me Jim or if you want to be formal then call me James. But enough of that sir shit."

"You know I will never call you by your name," I said. "I have to show some respect for the elders. Not like the bums here addressing everyone by their name. If it makes you feel old, then maybe its because you are old."

That always agitated the old timer. James Wakowski was in his late sixties. A heavy set guy around five foot nine.

A little shorter than me but looking much shorter since, like I had said to him many times, he had started growing horizontally in his older age. Had trouble pronouncing my name so he had decided to call me Pan, which meant Chief in Polish. Yes, he was one of the buddies I had made working at that grocery store.

"Whatever," he said as he sat in the chair by the ice freezer. It was my idea to put a chair there so the old timers, who liked to hang around and bullshit with me, had a place to rest while venting their frustrations.

"Anyway, what is new?" he said leaning back against the freezer.

"Well, I think I am in love," I thought but chose not to say. Instead I just said," Not much, how about you?"

"Same old shit," he said. "Well I haven't seen you in almost a month so tell me what's new on the movie front."

Everybody knew that I was a big movie buff. Weekends were spent down at the movie theater at the Menlo Park Mall.

They had a nice big theater there. Ten screens and it was wide open once you bought a ticket and stepped in. It was just so easy to theater hop. I would go there before noon on a Friday night, buy a ticket for a matinee, and then just go from one movie to another. Another good thing was that you could smoke outside in the area where the concession stand was. So I would watch one movie, come out and have a cigarette, get some popcorn or something, and then go into another movie. There were many days when I would spend around ten to twelve hours in there.

I ended up watching three or more movies, and step out of there when it was close to midnight or later. "How do you do it?", a lot of people would ask me. A couple of times, I had gone with friends and they just couldn't make it. They said their "asses" were hurting after all that sitting.

But I, honest to God, didn't care or mind.

"Well, I have seen a bunch of movies," I said. "The Scarlet Letter, Jade, Strange Days. I have to go home and check what I saw."

"Anything good?" he asked.

"Well, The Scarlet Letter was terrible. But I knew that going in. Just went to see it because Demi Moore was supposed to be naked in it. I think I may have fallen asleep and missed that part. Jade was okay. But Strange Days was awesome. Loved it."

"Oh, yeah. Who's in that?" Jim asked.

"Ralph Fiennes," I said.

Jim just shook his head indicating he had no idea who that was.

"Well, do you know who Angela Basset is?"

"No," said Jim.

"How about Julliette Lewis?"

"No," came the response.

"Okay, then do you know who Humphrey Bogart is?" I said.

Finally, the old man's face lit up as he heard a name he recognized.

"Oh, yeah. I know Bogie," he said smiling cheerfully.

"Well," I replied, "he's not in it."

Jim started to laugh as I told him I just wanted to see if anything would register in his Polish head.

"You are good, Pan," he said laughing. "That's why I like you."

Then some guy came in for a pack of cigarettes and I stood up to give him his smokes, as my mind started to drift off and think about Marya again. Damn it, this was getting to be too much.

But thinking about her was suddenly interrupted by a realization. A realization that maybe I was starting to lose touch with everything else around me.

Constant thoughts of her were making me realize that I was pretty much fixated with her. Everything else was blurry. Which may be why I had just told the old man Jim about a bunch of movies that I had seen a couple of years ago. No, it was not intentional. I had gone to the Menlo Park movie theater over the weekend but changed my mind about my theater hopping ritual.

I had seen nothing. Maybe if I had seen something, it would have been a healthy escape for my mind. But I didn't see anything. And I didn't feel like getting into it with Jim. So I had just regurgitated a movie-going experience from the past. Hell, the old man didn't know what was new at the movies, anyway.

Chapter 32

"Are you okay?" Taya Ji said as I walked in the door.

"Yes," I said. "Why do you ask?"

"I don't know. You look like something is bothering you."

Something bothering me would be an understatement. But he didn't have to know.

"No, sir, I am fine," I said taking off my backpack and dropping it to the floor.

"Just checking, beta ji. How did it go today?"

"It was okay, I guess. Not too many people came," I said taking out the two hundred rupees I had made for the day. If that sounds like a lot, then let me say that it was nothing.

Four letters read and three written. That was pretty bad. The people had just given me what they had and I had not asked for any more or less. Anyway, Taya Ji had told me never to ask for a certain amount.

Just take what was given and that is what I did.

"Who came?" he asked.

The old man was staying home but his mind was still stuck at the train station. He probably sat around in my absence and thought about "his" people. I had told him to go over to Khan's Canteen and hang around there. At least he could chat with some people there or watch TV...at least do something.

"Did you go to Khan's today?" I asked totally ignoring what he had asked me.

"Yes, I went there for a little while. Had a cup of tea and talked to him about the problems of the world and how we could solve them."

"Any luck?" I asked.

He just smiled and shook his head. Then he realized that I had never given his question an answer.

"So who came?"

I squatted down on the floor and leaned against the wall.

"Qureshi sahib brought a letter from his son in Karachi. Noor Bibi had to have a letter written to her son. I don't think she likes her daughter-in-law. And then there were a couple of others. Can I just rest a little for now? I will think of who else came," I said, this time closing my eyes.

"Of course, beta ji. Rest first and then there's some nan cholay in the plate over there."

"That sounds good," I said as I started to get more horizontal on the floor. I like nan cholay. Cholay were chick peas and the nan was a flat bread that usually lost its charm if you didn't eat it hot and straight out of the tandoor, the clay ovens that they were made in, baked over an open flame. If you let them cool off, they lost the crunch that I was a big fan of since childhood. But it was food.

I put my arm under my head, closed my eyes, and tried not to let my mind stray in the direction where it was probably going to head.

Chapter 33

"So what did you people think?" Mr Jones said leaning against his desk.

It was the day after we had gone to see Schindler's List. Spielberg's epic about the Holocaust had come out the past year and the State wanted all the kids in schools to see it. Of course, the school had gone for the cheapest movie theater that they could get.

We had gone to the ramshackle one on Elmira Avenue in Elizabeth. The place was dank, dreary, and depressing regardless of what you were watching. It could be a cheerful musical or a depressing opus like the one we had seen. Sitting there watching the screen, you would feel depressed anyway. So our World History class had ended up in that place and the popcorn was not included. But with all the multiplexes popping up all around us, that theater wasn't going to last long. It was a little sad, but the movie had been sadder.

"That sex scene was awesome," Joey said from the back of the class.

Mr. Jones frowned and shook his head, "See, its a great movie but I don't understand why they had to make it so graphic."

I think it was time for me to say something. "I think it was necessary."

"Of course, all you guys thought it was great," Jen decided to comment while rolling her eyes.

"No," Mr. Jones said, "it wasn't necessary. In old movies, everything was implied. A little left to the imagination."

He must have been close to sixty, but he was still teaching. Must have had some passion for the job. Or still needed the second income since his wife worked at some department store.

"No," I said, "I think that it worked better with the scene being so graphic."

"Yeah," Joey said from his seat again, "that chick was hot. Nice rack and all."

"Be quiet, Joseph," Mr. Jones said. You knew he was getting angry since he addressed Joey by his full name. Then he turned his eyes to me, "Now why do you think that it had to be so graphic? And I don't want to hear any of the garbage like I just heard from that one," he pointed to Joey.

"Well," I said, "I don't think it would have worked that well if we had just seen Schindler picking up the woman at some bar and then just saying farewell to her the morning after. We would have had to figure what had happened and it just wouldn't have the same effect. We actually got to see what happened and it kind of put things in perspective about how he operated and the kind of person he was… It just kind of makes you look at the guy in a certain way. And then what he proceeds to do with saving the lives of those people and wishing he could have done more. I don't know but I just think that if we hadn't seen him doing that woman in that graphic manner, his deeds later on wouldn't have seemed so noble. That's how I took it."

"Hmmm," Mr. Jones pondered for a moment, "I guess it could be taken that way. But any other comments besides that sex scene?"

There was silence for a few seconds and then Brian said from the back of the room," All those head shots were pretty cool." Then he realized what he had just said and tried to clarify what he meant," I mean, it was bad about those people getting killed and all but it was pretty *bad-ass* how those people were shown getting shot up."

Mr. Jones sighed and I leaned back in my chair thinking that maybe taking a bunch of tenth graders to that movie wasn't such a great idea.

Mr. Jones wasn't alone in thinking that it wasn't such a great idea to show kids that movie.

After all, ours was a generation that had been desensitized to violence. We had grown up watching cartoons where that sort of violence was inflicted on cartoon characters. But that had been all in good fun. Jerry the mouse going after Tom the cat and finding all kinds of ingenious ways of torturing that feline. So we didn't care when we saw those atrocities on screen when we had already seen Jason Voorhees doing a lot worse to horny adolescents. So how were we supposed to differentiate between what happened at those summer camps and what happened in those concentration camps. It wasn't really all our fault. Maybe it was the parents. Maybe it was society. Who the hell was I to sit there, trying to decide who to blame for our mental inability to grasp the horrors that men brought on their fellow men? After all, I had been a big fan of gory horror movies. I went out of my way looking for Silent Night, Deadly Night to see a psycho dressed as Santa bring horrors instead of presents. Sure, the movie was pretty terrible but some of the killings were pretty creative. Thank God, I had not become desensitized to the point where violence just seemed like a fun distraction on the screen. I actually even cried a little when I was watching Schindler's List.

Thank God for the darkness of the movie theater and its ability to cloak my shame.

Chapter 34

Whatever happened between Marya and I? Nothing actually. No, we didn't get intimate. I didn't even kiss the girl.

So how the hell could I say I was in love with her? I have no idea how to explain it. I think I mentioned before that I am not a *pro* in the ladies department. I was hardly anything at all in that department.

So it was just a feeling. A feeling that I wanted to be with this person. A feeling that I decided to categorize as love. It was something that I had never felt. It was something that I realized could be the L-word. How else to define that unrecognizable urge to be with someone? Yes, it had to be love.

That four-letter word that I had been unfamiliar with but had heard a lot about. This is it, I decided. I love that girl. She is the one for me. What I didn't factor into the whole equation was whether I was the one for her.

❧

"Is this the closest place where you can check out cds and stuff?" Marya said.

"No, actually there's been a change in plans," I said. "The truth is that I have a few friends I would like you to meet. I like you, and I think you should like me."

The look on her face changed to one of apprehension.

"Are you serious?" she managed to say after a little hesitation.

"Yes," I said. Then, "No, I am just kidding. I am sorry if that was in bad taste, which I am thinking that it was.

No, there are plenty of places around here that you can go for cds and stuff. I am just taking you to the one that I like. Yes, its a little farther but, for some reason, I started to like it there. So I always go there."

"Okay, I am just a tourist. You are the guide," she said.

I realized that she may be a little cold since I had the window cracked down a little so my smoke could go out and not annoy my passenger.

I threw the cigarette out and rolled the window up.

"Sorry," I said.

"For what?" she asked.

I decided not to go into an explanation. Just looked at the road ahead and then gave her another look, followed by a smile. Yes, I liked this girl.

But I was so damn stupid. Stupid, stupid, stupid, I thought to myself. I should have never said that thing about taking her to a few friends. That was incredibly stupid. Yes, I was just kidding around. And I hoped that she knew that. But even if she did know that, she would still be a skeptical about the kind of mind frame that would joke around like that. Yes, I was incredibly stupid. But like I said before, I was new to this arena. I had no idea how to behave. I had plenty of girl friends but never a girlfriend.

Chapter 35

"You look tired? Did you rest okay?" Taya Ji asked.

"I am fine. Just a little headache," I said.

Of course, I was not okay. I felt like shit. I had trouble sleeping all night. I had gotten used to sleeping on the hard floor with just a sheet between me and the ground. No, it wasn't that. It was just my head full of ghosts, thoughts, and fears. As I had put my head down on the flattened pillow at night, the first thoughts that came to me were of Marya Durani. I wondered how she was doing. Probably married by now. Or still waiting for that big day. Still planning. Because in Pakistan, weddings were pretty extravagant. In the US, there were only a few people invited to weddings. In Pakistan, weddings were huge. People ended up inviting everyone they could… family, friends, friends of the family, friends of the friends, and pretty much everyone that had gotten a whiff of the bride, the groom, or their families. It wouldn't be uncommon to have close to a hundred people at the wedding. At least, that is what I had witnessed at the few weddings I had attended as a child.

I hated going to weddings. Plus, it wasn't a one day affair. Usually, three or four days. One day would be the groom's turn. Another day would be the bride's turn. Then there would be a common day where they would finally end up being pronounced husband and wife. Plus this could all be preceded by a Mehndi, where all the females gathered around and partied away. The "mehndi" was not only the title of the occasion but also a key ingredient. Mehndi was what Westerners had gotten to know as "Henna." That stuff that, mostly females, ended up putting on their hands in decorative patterns... a temporary tattoo of sorts. Anyway, that is why weddings were a big affair. And that is why I thought that Marya was probably still in the planning stages.

So I had been thinking of her before falling asleep. Then I had started thinking of the other Marya who had come to me at the train station.

The one who had been hesitant about having me read or write any of her letters. It must have been well past midnight, when I probably fell asleep. And then the azaan woke me up around five in the morning. But I should have been used to that.

Allah Akbar, it began and there went my sleep. The azaans were the "call to prayer for all people." The men would rush over to the nearest masjid, or mosque, while the women said their prayers at home. Each area had a couple of mosques, at least. You could probably find three or more within a square mile. And they all had these speakers where you could hear the mullahs calling the people to their prayers, five times a day.

And Allah Akbar is how the azaan began, and that phrase was repeated a few times in the entirety of the azaan. *Allah Akbar. Allah is great.*

One of the reasons why I had started turning away from Islam. My God was great but my God did not need to tell his people to constantly praise him.

My God was thanked by me, every waking moment because I wanted to thank him and not because he demanded that I thank him. Just like life itself.

I didn't help anyone and demand they thank me. Because that is what my God told me. *Do whatever I could but not because I would expect anything in return.*

And that was my God. And that is why I would probably be categorized as a "kafir" or non believer. Sure, but the only thing was that I did believe in something.

❦

One of the hardest things in my life had been to tell my parents that I wasn't a Muslim.

Where have we failed, they must have asked themselves.

From a young age, I had started reciting the Koran. A tutor came to the house and had me read the Holy Book every day. When I got to the age of seven, saying my prayers five times a day became a requirement. I would lay out the prayer mat five times a day and do as I had been taught. When I got older, I would run to the nearby mosque, whenever I could, and say my prayers with the other men and boys.

It was all good.

But things kept bothering me about my faith and I started to do what I had been told never to do. I started asking questions. I wanted to know why I could do certain things and why I couldn't do other things. That was easy for the elders to explain. Then things got more complex. Why do I have to read the Quran in Arabic? It wasn't my language. Why couldn't I read it in Urdu, the language I had grown up speaking, reading, and writing? Because if you read the translation, it will lose some of its meaning, is what I was told. It didn't make sense to me but years later when I was in the US, I discovered how things lose some meaning, no matter how well you do it, in translation. Fine, so I was supposed to learn Arabic and then read the Quran.

But why do we have to pray five times a day?

So we can thank Allah for all his blessings. But shouldn't we thank him because we feel that we should and not because he demands it from us. And why does he demand we constantly praise him? Isn't that wrong according to Islam? To ask another to praise you, whatever the term for that is. Isn't that a little immodest? Isn't modesty the better path? And why can men have four wives but women can't have four husbands? That goes back in time when the men were dying in wars and leaving their wives without any support. A man could marry up to four women but had to make sure that he could treat each one equally and provide her with all she needed. In other words... help out the widows left by the wars. But why marry them? Why couldn't you just help someone in need? Why did you have to marry her? And you had to be married to the one you were sleeping with.

Monogamy sounded fair.

But what about those promises of the afterlife? In heaven, a man who had lived a good life, would be rewarded with so many virgins.

What about the women who lived a good life?

Anyway, I was looking for a way out of my upbringing. I didn't feel that I needed the shackles of religion to be a good person.

However, I always thanked my God for showing me what had to be done. That is why I was not a kafir in my eyes.

Chapter 36

How did I come to think that I was in love with Marya? I think I mentioned earlier that this was a new terrain for me. I had never gotten into this whole thing with girls. So, I couldn't really blame anyone for thinking was I gay or whispering "fag" behind my back. I had come to the US to get an education… Sorry, let me correct myself there. I had been sent to the United States to get an education. The education system back in Pakistan wasn't that great. Actually, most of the systems over there were no good. Be it the legal system or any other system you could think of, name, or devise. The place was a den of corruption.

All that mattered was who you knew. You could have a Masters degree and a PhD but if you didn't know anybody where you were looking to work, your diplomas were more worthless than used toilet paper. Which is why you would run into these people working in offices who wouldn't even know how to read while an educated person might be sweeping the floors of the same office. That is how things were. Which is why my parents had decided that an American education would do me good. Or I could have gone to London. But they didn't have any relatives or acquaintances in London and a young male without a chaperone wasn't such a great idea. So I had come to the US and had been quietly earnest about fulfilling my parents' wishes.

One of their main concerns had been that I would get distracted by the females, that I would get into the whole American tradition of getting myself a girlfriend. This, in their eyes, was a big reason why America was falling off the track while other countries were advancing. You can see, they had told me, foreigners take most of the good jobs like doctors and lawyers. Americans, whom they saw as the white people, are just not up to doing those kinds of things. So finish your studies, get a good job, and we will find you a nice Pakistani girl was what they said. And I went along with it. This is why I never had a girlfriend. She would just hold me back.

I tried not to fall, but couldn't help tripping when I met Marya.

She was pretty. She was intelligent. And, I guess, somewhere in the back of my mind, she was the safest one. One that would not disappoint my family, since she was Pakistani. Hell, I was getting older and couldn't help feeling the way I did.

My first thought was that I just liked her. But what made me categorize it as love was the constant thoughts that interrupted my life. I couldn't do anything without thinking of her. What will she think? Will she like it? If she was here, then what would I do? If she were here, how would I do it? Why can't she be here right now? I wish she was here. Then we could do this. Or we could do that. God damn it, I want her to be here with me. Or, I want to be there with her. And I want it like that day after day.

I want to be with her.

I figured this was what they had meant by love. I had read about it. I had heard about it. And now I was in the middle of it. This should be interesting.

I realized that I had fallen for the girl when I got home from the diner that first night.

Love at first sight? A bunch of bullshit. It was just something that my brain had started figuring while the heart was running free. You know the heart thing… If you don't then I hope you will someday.

"She wasn't bad looking," said Dan at Josh's Pub when I accidentally slipped after having more than what I usually had. That was the first sign that something was going on. All the people near me had given me a look when I asked Josh to fill my rocks glass with some more RumpleMinze.

Then I had just turned to Dan, who was the nearest one, and started telling him about how I was starting to feel.

"Yeah, dude, you need to get laid," he continued.

"It's not like that," I tried to explain. "I think I really, really liked her. Maybe that other L-word.

Maybe I am even in love with her."

Dan took a couple of quiet puffs from his cigarettes, put it down in the miserable looking ashtray on the bar, and said, "Dude, that's a little fucked-up. How can you say you love her. You barely know her. So you know her name and that she is from Pakistan. I mean, I was doing Jen for a few months and I still couldn't say that I was in love with her. Sure, I used to say that to her but you know how things are. And you barely know this chick. Hell with screwing her, did you even kiss her?"

I was just sitting there thinking that I should have never divulged this information to this guy. Especially when he had been there for quite a while. He had no possible way of understanding what I was going through. Even if he was sober, he wouldn't understand.

I shook my head and said, "well, we shook hands when she was leaving. I know that means nothing here in the US but in Pakistan, men and women don't shake hands."

"Oh, yeah, that means a shit load," Dan said.

I just got up and went over to the jukebox with a crumpled up single. Halfway there, I realized that the thing would never accept it.

I turned back and got a nicer looking bill from my money that was sitting on the bar. That is how things worked at Josh's. You just left your money on the bar and left whatever was an appropriate tip when time came to leave. I think that is how things worked at most bars...

I wouldn't know since this was my only watering hole.

"Dude," Josh said in a loud voice, as I stood there looking at the selection and figuring out what to play, "go for it."

I just nodded and decided to play Paint It Black from The Rolling Stones. It just seemed appropriate for the way I was feeling.

The music came on and I realized I had to pick two more songs since you got three for a dollar. I tried to pick something else but had a hard time thinking. So I just went back to my stool and said in a loud voice, "there's two more choices left if anybody wants to play something."

Nothing happened for a while and then some girl from the other end of the bar stumbled over to the jukebox.

"You like the Stones?" Josh said.

"They aren't bad," I said, glad that a different topic had come up.

Chapter 37

So that was all I did sitting at my table at the train station. It wasn't like there were a lot of people who wanted their stuff read or written. Most had graduated to the next level of communication- telephones. However, not many called outside of the country. And not just because it was expensive. Many people didn't have phones in their homes. They would usually go to someone they knew who had a phone, and hoped that they would be allowed to make their call.

Sure, people had phones in their homes but not the people I was dealing with. Some of these people didn't even have electricity. Let's just say that wealth wasn't distributed evenly in Pakistan. Some had so much and some had nothing.

But getting back to what I did at my table. I did pretty much nothing. I sat there and waited for someone to show up and until they did, I just smoked and read. However, no matter what I did, I couldn't help thinking. Thinking about where I was, where I had been, and where I planned to go. That last one was still blurry. And all the thinking was always accompanied by thoughts of her. Marya. I wasn't kidding when I said I was in love with the girl. I, honest to God and without any choice in the matter, had fallen for her. Now the only thing was to find a way to flush out all memories of her. And that wasn't about to happen so easily.

ॐ

When I had left the diner that night, I had my mind set on the notion that this was going to be my girl. What came first? The notion that I was in love with her, or the idea that I should be in love with her? I have no idea. Maybe it was the later because I did give it time. Remember? When she wanted me to take her to buy some cds, I took her to the store that was further away. Why? So I could know her better. So I could find out some more about her. Did I?

ॐ

"So how do you like it here?" I asked.

"It's nice. I guess," Marya replied.

"What do you mean by guessing?" I asked. "Either you like it or you can't stand it."

She smiled and then said," I mean that its good for me. But I am just visiting. I will be going back soon. I have no idea what its like to actually live here. From what I have seen, everybody is working their asses off."

I nodded, keeping an eye on the road ahead and smoking by cigarette. Sure, I had thrown one out, concerned that the draft from the slightly open window may be to cold for this cute little foreigner in the next seat. But then I had decided to turn up the heat and put the window down just a little.

"Maybe that is why America is way ahead of Pakistan," I said. "Because people actually work here. The weekends are for relaxing. Maybe if there was this kind of system in Pakistan, the country wouldn't be in such bad shape."

'Yeah," she replied staring out her window.

She had done quite a lot of shopping at CD Turf…spent a little over a hundred dollars on cds. Some albums and a couple of singles.

In my opinion, she had good taste in music since a lot of the stuff she bought was the kind of stuff I liked. U2, Stabbing Westward, and more. None of the teenybopper crap that was hip those days --- Backstreet Boys or, even worse in my eyes, Puff Daddy.

"So what do you do in Pakistan?" I asked.

"Nothing really," she said. "What can a girl do over there? I convinced my parents to let me get a job at this friend's agency. They do promotions and stuff for banks and companies. I didn't care about the money. Just wanted a distraction from the home life. So that was good. It gave me a little experience and some spending money. Still don't know what that experience is going to do for me since I don't think I will be going any further on my own."

So we talked about the banalities of life. About what we were planning to do in our respective futures....and about what we had accomplished so far.

About what we had wanted to accomplish. About our vain attempts at gaining independence. She would be okay since her parents were probably going to take care of her needs and responsibilities.

I, on the other hand, felt that I was pretty screwed. Where the heck was I headed, I asked myself like so many other times. But this time it was serious since I had to have something to show if I was going to marry this girl. Marry this girl? Of course. Because by this point I had realized that I really liked her. That I was, just maybe, in love with Marya Durani.

Of course, she had not hinted at anything about what her friend would tell me in a few days.

Chapter 38

I was bored out of my mind. Nobody was coming to my table. Nobody needed to write to anyone? What about getting a letter read? Something? Anything? I had gone through half a pack of cigarettes already.

What else could I do? There was that other option but it scared me because I didn't want to go there. That option wasn't really a choice. I could sit there and think. Reading wasn't working out because I just couldn't get myself to concentrate. Halfway through a sentence I would forget what I was reading and when I did recall, after some effort, I would forget where I was on the page. It was a collection of Stephen King short stories. Nightmares and Dreamscapes. I found short stories were more apt for the mental stage I was going through. Going through, I hoped, and not a stage I had graduated to. Novels just didn't hold my interest. I would lose track halfway through and start to forget what it was that I had gotten through.

And this, coming from someone who had managed to start and finish The Brothers Karamazov in tenth grade.

Things just weren't the same. Something had changed. And not for the better, I was afraid.

Then I felt someone approaching my table. I looked up from my book and couldn't help but smile and thank God it was her. It was Marya. No, not Marya Durani. Marya Sajid. My new ailment, I was afraid.

"Hello," she said, smiling and taking a seat across from me. Then she opened up her purse and pulled out a letter.

So she finally thought she could trust me.

"Hello," I said, smiling and reaching for the letter.

She had a green colored shalwar kameez on. What most women had on around those parts. The shalwar kameez and not necessarily green. Although jeans and t-shirts were also getting to be pretty common now. Those had actually become a status symbol of sorts.

Having jeans on meant that you were a more modern female. No longer held back by what the society had dictated for so long.

Of course, the mullahs, or elders, didn't appreciate this change in females. So she had shalwar kameez on and the obligatory dupata, or sheet, covering her head. It was supposed to convey modesty and keep the males from ogling the passing females. In my opinion, that

didn't quite work out as planned because the men would give women dressed like that more thorough looks. They had to work harder with their imaginations in stripping away all that was covered. At least that is how I thought of it. There was no stopping the male animal.

I had never been one to stare at females. Even in the US, when all was on display during the hot summer months, I found it to be a little rude to stare at women.

But then, I was labeled a fag by many over there. But I didn't care then or now.

So her black dupata was covering her head since the hair was supposed to be completely covered by all females. I never did get that.

Believe it or not, the way she was dressed could still be considered immodest by some. Many women wore burqas. Those covered them from head to toes, leaving only a small slot on the face for the eyes. That, in my opinion, was a little conceited, to think you were that gorgeous, which many of those women were definitely not. How did I know? Well, I had seen some of these burqa clad women without their coverings when I was a kid. Nope, definitely nothing worth hiding, I had thought.

❦

But getting back to Marya. She had put the letter before me and I had picked it up slowly because I was a little distracted by how she looked. Did I mention she was beautiful? Because she was. Light skin, brown eyes, and brown hair that would have come to her shoulders if it weren't tied up with a rubber band behind her neck. She must have been around nineteen or twenty years old, right around my age.

What she said next was something I should have been prepared for. But it was something that still made my mind skip a little.

"It's from my husband," she said.

That's right, she was married. I knew that. Then what was I so shocked at? It was going to surface its ugly head one of these days.

"Okay, then let's see what he says," I said smiling.

I was a bad person. That's all I could think. How could I even be thinking of this girl in the way I was thinking? How could I be even hoping of sweeping her off her feet? Yes, that was a clichéd expression but one I was leaning on constantly when I met someone of the opposite gender. Actually, not always. Only when I thought this could be the one. In other words, this was only the second time I had thought of it and, incidentally, both the females involved had been named Marya.

This time, I was not just thinking of sweeping her off her feet but rescuing her. Rescuing her from a lousy marriage. Probably a lousy arranged marriage that her family had forced upon her. After all this was a girl, twenty or so, who was married to some guy more than twice her age - oh, I am sorry, did I forget to mention that this Sajid fellow was in his forties? Because he was. But that is how many arranged marriages wound up. Parents, eager to rid themselves of a burden that was a daughter, giving her away to any possible matches that came by. And it didn't even matter if it was a "match." As long as it was a male looking to get married.

And, I was guessing, Marya and Sajid had probably had a few weeks of marital bliss before he had set off to go overseas for a better job - so he could provide her with more.

Then he was going to come back with a lot of money and the two could get started on starting a family. Have a few kids, preferably boys, and be on their way to a happy future.

A bunch of bullshit. Yes, I didn't take too kindly to this system of doing things. But it was years and years of tradition. Who was I to come around and challenge the way things were?

Right now, I had a job to do. A letter to read and maybe another to write.

I was furious. But only on the inside. On the outside, I opened the envelope and calmly pulled the sheet of paper that was enclosed.

"Okay, then," I began reading the thing.

Chapter 39

I always felt guilty. I hated myself. I didn't like the way I thought. I always thought there was something wrong with me. A little fucked up. I tried to find some way of correcting myself. And if that wasn't possible then maybe there was a way I could punish myself. To put it simply, I thought there was something wrong with the way I thought. And it was never more evident than when I started thinking about Jennie.

She was a blonde in my biology class at Ridgewood High School. Now we are talking about ninth grade when I was fifteen years old. She was actually fourteen and had been put in that class because she was gifted or however else they chose to classify it. In my eyes, she was gifted in other ways. She was damn hot. She had this beautiful face accompanied by an equally gorgeous body.

I would look at her, but never too obviously. It was hard not to when she would be dressed for the weather in the hot summer months. But I think it was normal for a guy to notice her. I noticed her. But what bothered the hell out of me was the fact that she was stuck in my head the way I had first seen her.

When she was fourteen. Because her family had moved away during that year. But she was stuck in my head the way I had seen her. She didn't age in my mind.

I would always think of her the way I had seen her at fourteen years of age and that disturbed the hell out of me. Why? Because I was getting older. Seventeen, eighteen, nineteen. But why was my mind fixated on this fourteen year old? I had to find a way out. I didn't want to be like that.

I wanted to find somebody around my age. So, in a way, that could be a reason why I had so eagerly fallen for Marya when I had met her. But I didn't want to think of it as being so simple. I didn't want to think that what I categorized as love, was simply a way out of thoughts that were starting to feel a little perverted. No, I had really fallen in love with Marya Durani.

But what the hell was wrong with me? Why did I always fall for those who were not that easy? My excuse with Marya Durani could be that I had no prior knowledge about her getting married. Fine - not my fault. If it was anybody's fault, it was hers, for never letting on that she was to be married. If anything, the bitch had led me on. And I hated myself for that. For calling her a bitch when it wasn't her fault at all. No, it was my entire fault. For looking into things that were not there. For seeing signs when there were none present. Was it wishful thinking? After all, the heart is a lonely hunter. Yes, it was my fault.

❧

It was always my fault. Because now I was falling for Marya Sajid, the innocent creature who had come to me to get her letters read. Who had trusted me to do something that she was unable to do. She didn't lead me on. I knew she was married. Then why the hell was I seeing her in a way that was definitely not right. That was just plain wrong.

How can you expect someone with a head full of demons like mine to ever be at peace? Which is why I didn't get too much sleep. Or rest for that matter. Of all the battlefields men may conquer, their mind is the most deceptive. Maybe because its always right there. Always with you. How I wish there was some way of leaving it behind.

❧

It would have never worked out with Jennie anyway. How would I know since I never even tried anything? No, it wasn't fear. And it sure as hell wasn't a lack of confidence. I think I mentioned before that one of the things I was most proud of was having a confident attitude. I could lie with the straightest face and look a person straight in the eyes while doing so. I never backed down. I made sure my point, no matter how flawed, came across. Was it something to be proud of? I had no idea. So why didn't I make a move with Jennie? Because I had the foresight of knowing that it would never work out. My family could never accept her. To them she would always be the witch who cast a spell on their innocent and naive son. Because no matter who made the move in the Pakistani parents' eyes, it was always the "white skinned witches" who trapped their sons with their charms. So that is why I didn't try anything with Jennie or anyone else, for the matter. Because I didn't want to disappoint my family.

Which is why it was so easy to label me a fag. And I didn't want to go into any explanations. It was much simpler just being labeled a fag.

So Marya Durani was such a safe bet. God forbid, I didn't want to think of her in that fashion...as a safe bet. It was the synchronicity of the way things happened. My lonely self, looking for someone while not admitting to myself that I was either looking or lonely. But sometimes it takes finding something to make one realize that you were looking for it.

I had gone to Karachi before I ended up moving in with Taya Ji in Pindi. That is exactly where Marya was from. I had her phone number and I kind of knew where she lived - an area known as Defense Society. They had pretty nice houses there. People living there had money. How they came about a lot of it was another story. Some had worked for it and earned it. Others, well there was a lot of unorthodox ways of coming across a fortune in Pakistan. But I wasn't there to question how or why she had her fortune. I just wanted to see her. I knew it wasn't going to do shit. I just wanted to see her. One more time.

"Can you take me to this address?" I said to the cab driver showing him the slip of paper with the address scribbled on it.

He gave it a thorough look and then looked at me. I hadn't gotten time to get to the money exchange. So I opened up my wallet and pulled out a ten dollar bill.

The guy's eyes lit up as he saw the bill. I didn't even know what the exchange rate was in those days but knew the ten bucks were worth a few hundred rupees, a worthwhile investment for the guy.

"Sure, sir," he said getting out of the driver's side and heading towards the back to open the door for me.

"Its okay," I said opening the back door and throwing my bag in the backseat.

Taxis in Pakistan, in my opinion, didn't really have a pleasant color. Yellow and black. But what the hell was I thinking? Its not like the yellow cabs back in the US were much more appealing to the eyes. The important thing was they got you around.

The guy pulled into the heavy traffic and I just had to admire the way he wove in and out of traffic to get to where he wanted. The systematic way of traffic in the US had spoiled me.

I just didn't remember the way things had been in Pakistan. No rules and survival of the fastest. The Hell with the traffic lights. If you could get through, you got through. Colors didn't matter. Red, yellow, or green.

Nobody gave a crap. And this guy was no different.

I finally gave a sigh of relief when he pulled into a calmer residential neighborhood.

This must be where she lived, I thought to myself as we started passing some very nice looking houses that had to be classified as mansions.

"This is it, sir," he said stopping in front of a huge two story beige house. Like most houses, there was a metal gate at end of the driveway. Through the rails, you could see a couple of cars parked in the driveway. Hondas; which were very common and almost a status symbol there. There were a couple of tall trees by the wall, and the lawn was nicely landscaped with rose bushes bordering the outline.

"Do you want me to go ring the bell?" the driver asked.

"No," I said after a brief pause. "You can take me back to the airport now."

He gave me a strange look and then just nodded.

So this is where she lived. At least until now. Soon she was getting married and moving on.

Nice, I thought to myself.

Chapter 40

Maybe stalkers were just shy. They didn't know what to say or do when it got down to it.

More justifications for my actions? No. I really thought so. I am not painting myself as too sympathetic a person, am I?

Falling for a soon-to-be married girl. Drinking away in bars. Thinking of a girl when she was only sixteen. Starting to fall for someone who was already married. Shattering my parents' dreams.

And now sympathizing with stalkers. Well, maybe I don't deserve sympathy. Maybe I should just deserve pity. And maybe that is all I was worthy of.

I have no idea how a straightforward cliché like myself would end up becoming what I did. A victim of circumstance? Just another way of justifying things.

Why was I sympathizing with stalkers, anyway? Because I was, in my opinion, doing just that.

I had asked Shazia for Marya's phone number. She didn't really want to give it to me.

"I have it written at home," she had said.

"Okay," I replied, "then can I have your number so I can call you and get it?"

I had "accidentally" run into her at the local supermarket.

"Sure," she said even though her demeanor was more of cautious reluctance.

And thus began what was, in my opinion, a form of stalking. I dialed that number so many times. Sometimes four or five times a day. I was considerate enough to factor in the ten-hour time difference. Pakistan was ten hours ahead --- about the only thing it was ahead in.

I would dial the number, usually from home, someone would pick up, and then I just hang up. A lot of times it would be some stranger's voice. Quite a few times, I knew it was Marya. Then I would think of what to say, come up blank, and hang up. What could I possibly say to change the inevitable? To make, what was to be… not be?

To alter the course of things? To make her fall for me the way I had fallen for her? There was no possible hope for me. To use an expression a friend used a lot, *I didn't have a snowball's chance in hell.*

And here's something else I did that will make me more of a sleazebag. After hanging up, I would call up the phone company and tell them that my call had been disconnected. They would check their computers and if they found the call to be less than sixty seconds, they would issue a credit.

"I do apologize," the operator would say.

"Its alright, I will try again," I said. Because I knew I was going to keep it up. And this being an international call, charges were going to pile up.

More justification for my unsympathetic actions. I am sorry, I meant pitiable actions.

Like I said a while back, I had given up on Islam. Just didn't touch me that way it did others. But I didn't consider myself a non-believer.

So I did step out of the circle of Islam. I didn't do anything that would make me seem like a Muslim. But I did pick up a few things while I was in that circle. I know that it doesn't make me seem too spiritual when I talk about my years as a Muslim as if it was a shopping trip. I ignored the things I didn't agree with, but I decided to hold on to the ones that appealed to me. Seems a little selfish. Or self-involved. Or anything else that can be associated with a "self" in front of it. Muslims are supposed to say their prayers five times a day. Thank Allah for everything and praise him. Its the latter that got to me. The praise. But what I did like about the prayers was the humility which was supposed to overcome one during the practice. Put you in your place. Reassure the fact that you were nothing compared to the greater scheme of things. How you bowed your head facing Mecca, regardless of where you were in the world.

The part that I liked the most was the "sijda." That is when you were kneeling on the ground and put your forehead on the ground. I kept that up. Not the entire namaaz. Just the sijda.

A few times a day, or whenever I had the chance, I would get on the ground, put my forehead to the ground, and thank the Lord for everything he had given me. Of course, I would also sneak in a few requests for what I needed. If it was possible for the Lord to bless me with those things, if they could be deemed appropriate. Never went too far, I thought. I didn't ask for much.

Didn't ask for money and didn't ask for luxuries. Just asked for the wisdom to know what was right and what was wrong. I asked for guidance. And asked for someone to end my lonely existence. That's it.

Humble, won't you say? I hoped so.

So that happened whenever it could. No prayer mat and no certain direction faced. Just me, my Lord, and the hope that nobody walked in on my daily ritual.

Chapter 41

"How would you like me to read it?" I asked Marya Sajid.

She gave me a blank look and then said," What do you mean?"

"I am sorry, I meant how did Taya Ji do it? Do you want me to read it word for word or do you want me to just read it and tell you what it says in my words," I said.

"Oh," she replied and started thinking. "Your taya just told me whatever it was about after

reading the entire thing. You can do whatever way you want."

"Okay," I said and started reading the thing.

How should I go about doing this, I thought to myself. After all, this was a husband writing to a wife, half a world away. What if there was some intimate stuff in it? Then I realized that this was Pakistan. There wasn't going to be any intimate stuff in that letter. I might as well just read the whole thing and then tell her what the gist of it was.

So this guy, her husband, had landed a comfy job as a waiter in some Pakistani/Indian restaurant. He was more of a busboy according to what he described as his duties - cleaning up after the customers left and setting up the table for the next arrival. But I wasn't about to tell her that her husband was a busboy. She wouldn't understand.

So it was a restaurant serving Pakistani and Indian food and under the same roof. It was surprising how these sworn enemies got along so well when they were far from their countries. All the animosities were left behind.

I had noticed that in the U.S., Indians and Pakistanis were like brothers . The hatred that existed between the two was nowhere to be seen. Maybe they were just more stoic about their hatred. Because, in those foreign countries, it was the white man that had to be watched out for... It didn't matter if you were a Muslim and your neighbor a Hindu. The skins were alike and the cultures pretty similar. After all, Indian movies did a lot better in Pakistan than Pakistani movies.

And music from those movies was what could probably be heard all around.

So I read the whole letter and it was all about how he was doing and what he was doing. How he liked it and how it got really cold there.

But he was okay. No mention of how he felt about being away from his wife. What an asshole, I thought to myself.

So I told Marya all that he had written.

"Is that it?" she said, smiling a strained smile like she was hoping for something more.

"Well," I started to say and hesitated about what I was going to say. "He says that he loves you very much and misses being away from you.

And he can't wait for the day he will see you again."

She had gotten up from the chair and was actually starting to leave. But then she froze and sat back down.

"He really said that?" she asked with a hesitant voice.

What the hell, I thought. I had started it so I might as well keep it up.

"Yes, he really said that," I replied thinking that it was probably something he had never said to this beautiful girl in person.

But it was something he should have said to her every waking moment. Cheesy, yes. But also the truth. What the hell did I know, though.

I just knew her from those few times I had met her. And all I knew about her was her name and a few tidbits about her personal life. For all I knew, she could be a super bitch. But I knew that wasn't true because no matter what the elders had told me, there was a lot that could be taken from a first impression. True, my first impression of her had been purely based on her physical appearance. She was definitely a head turner if she wasn't so modestly dressed.

Another reason why having women all covered up wasn't such a great idea. Because it made the imaginations of men go haywire. I, for example, hadn't seen much of her beyond her face but the mind kept thinking of what else was there. I hated myself for that. Here was a decent female trying to go about her life and I was thinking of her in a fashion that was not decent. But was it okay if it stayed within my head? If nobody else knew? That is how I justified it for myself. But then I realized that I was just an asshole trying to rationalize my behavior. But it was okay if it stayed within me and nobody else knew. No? Maybe. But I was still an asshole who didn't deserve the rationalized end. I hated myself.

"He never spoke to me like that," she said shyly. I think I was starting to embarrass her.

"Well," I said, "sometimes people find it easier to say certain things when they are not talking directly to the other person."

She was actually blushing now.

She had never expected this sort of thing to be in the letters. If she had known, she would have never brought them to me. But how could she have known.

"He never said that kind of thing before," she said, not looking at me directly.

"I don't know what to say," I said, because I really didn't know what to say. Why the hell did I say what I had said?

I had no idea. Maybe because I thought that it is what she deserved.

Chapter 42

In 1995 I realized that Powder was just what I needed. I had been going through this phase where my mood was always depressed. I felt miserable. I didn't know why. There was something wrong, somewhere.

I had no idea where. I just wanted to sit down and cry. But when I sat down, I didn't cry. Because I just couldn't.

There was no reason to.

Then why was this over powering sadness my constant companion.

Maybe I was depressed. I mean, I knew I was depressed but maybe it was a depression that had nothing to do with what was going on in my life. Maybe it was a chemical imbalance because I had read that a chemical imbalance in the brain could lead to these feelings of hopelessness.

The kind of feeling that was constantly clouding me. I needed something like Prozac. That was supposed to be good.

So I started talking to a few friends.

"Maybe Gina can hook you up," Doug said. "Her dad's a shrink so he's probably got that shit lying all over the house."

We were sitting at the Crosswood Diner on Route 22. It was a twenty-four hour place and bums like us were always welcome there. We just ordered a cup of coffee and sat there smoking and getting refills. We left a good tip though. Five or ten dollars for what we saw as being just hangers on.

Doug, one of my high school buddies who had started hanging out with me after school, was the only person I confided in about my mental predicament.

"Seriously, dude," he said, "why the fuck did you tell me that. I mean, its cool that you told me but I have to do something now. Otherwise, I'd feel responsible if you ended up slitting your wrists or something."

"No, that's a good idea. I will talk to Gina and see if she can hook me up with something," I said.

I wasn't going to. The last thing I wanted was for some girl to know about this.

And then I happened to watch Powder, a movie about some weird looking kid facing some tough times in his adolescence thanks to his weird looks and strange abilities. Honestly, I can't even remember what the movie was entirely about. All I knew was that it was the most depressing movie I had ever seen. Thank God, I had gone by myself to see it. It was a Tuesday matinee and there must have been about three other people in the entire theater.

And thank God, because nobody would see me crying over Powder's predicament.

Poor guy. How could his life be so cruel? But it was good. Because it helped me.

I sat in the dark and I cried.

That really doesn't sound too good, does it? But that is what was becoming of me and I didn't want to believe that it was merely some disproportion of chemicals in my brain that was dictating how life was. It had to be something more. Something more real. In the same dimension as me.

I smoked and smoked some more, thinking over what it could be. The only conclusion I came to was that it was the real world. Yes, it was the big evil world out there.

I was about to graduate high school and had no idea what I wanted to do or where I wanted to go. I wanted to stay in high school. It had taken me long enough to find some place where I was comfortable.

And I was only seventeen at the time. Everybody else was eighteen. I guess I had started school early in Pakistan since I had never skipped a grade. But later on in life, I would tell people that I had skipped a grade... It just made them look at me differently.

But they probably just thought I was some geek.

One good thing about leaving high school was that I could move out on my own. Leave my uncle and aunt and go solo. And it was college time. I didn't even apply to colleges too seriously.

It wasn't like I was doing bad in school or something. I was still in the top twenty in my class of 135 kids. I decided to go with what my guidance counselor suggested. If I wasn't sure about what to do or where to go then I should just go to the County college. I could do some general classes, find my calling, and then go on from there.

Because I didn't know what my calling was. According to my parents and family, I wanted to be a doctor. Everybody in Pakistan wanted their kid to be a doctor. How can you really expect a country full of doctors to go anywhere?

So in 1995, I graduated from high school and started going to the County college for a bunch of bullshit classes. But more importantly, I moved into my own place. A small apartment not too far from where I had lived with my uncle and aunt. My new place was in Kinsville, the town where I was going to end up working for the Patel's and discover my watering hole at Josh's Pub.

But getting back to my ever present and unexplainable misery. My search for more tear-jerkers didn't go too well.

Nothing ever got to me the way Powder did.

I hated that movie.

Chapter 43

I hoped to God it wasn't happening again. I mean, if it was going to happen then fine. But why did it have to happen with someone with the same name? There were plenty of other Pakistani females around. Why the hell did I have to start sense these feelings for another one named Marya? These feelings? What feelings? I had no idea. But I was starting to think about Marya Sajid the same way I had started to think about Marya Durani back in the US. Yes, me and my damned mind. Great choice, buddy. At least with Marya Durani, I could say that I had no idea she was set to be married. But this one I knew was already married and her husband was twice her age and nowhere near.

That didn't justify how I felt. And I hardly knew her. All I knew about her was how she looked. Yes, she was beautiful but that didn't mean anything. Was I that superficial? Maybe I was just frustrated and wanted someone, regardless of who, what or where.

Okay, so there was no denying I was frustrated. Sexually? I had no idea. What I did know was that I was frustrated, sick, and tired. Of what? A lot actually...

Of being the nice guy who always finished last. Why couldn't I have a girl? I was nice and honest to them. Is that why I was being nice? So I could get into their pants? Because if that was the case than I was no better than the guys they ended up going out with. At least those guys were honest about their intentions. I, when I thought over it, was actually worse for putting up a facade to get to them. But I wasn't putting up a facade. What I said, I meant, and what I meant, I said. But nobody knew that.

It was all within me. Only I knew of my intentions and honesty. Telling somebody was just a self congratulatory thing. Was I sure about this one? Of course. But then I had also been sure about the other one. The biggest problem was finding a way of getting around her being married. What the hell was I thinking when I added that thing towards the end of her husband' letter about loving her and missing her.

He didn't write that in the letter. He probably would never write that kind of thing. He probably wouldn't even say something like that.

So what the hell was I thinking, telling her something that wasn't even there? All I could think of was, God help me.

And when I got home, I cried, because I had no idea what was happening once again. It was just like the first time, which I had sworn would be the last time. But just as I had been helplessly adrift that first time, I was getting swept up into this shit again.

It is your time to study and get a good career, I had been told many times by the parents and other "grown-ups" in Pakistan. When you have gotten settled, we will find you a nice wife and then you can start a family.

That was the wisdom passed around in Pakistan. Do everything in a systematic way.

But life wasn't that systematic. The way I saw it, you got a bunch of shit thrown at you, and life became what you ended up with after sifting through it. That was my outlook.

But Islam teaches you all the right ways of doing things. If you don't stray from what that is teaching you, you won't get caught in all the troubles that it is shielding you from… Its all for your own good. Sure, it all made sense to these people who had followed unquestioningly and never strayed from it. But I, honest to God, had been helpless in the whole situation. To me, it was God who made me question everything.

So it must be God who led me astray. Why? Because he wanted me to find the truth my own way.

That is what I thought. Then why did it all hurt so much?

It seemed so right when I met Marya in the United States. She was going to be the one. And my parents were going to be so happy that they had trusted their son.

And he was going to marry a Pakistani girl.

But that went nowhere. And now I was in Pakistan and found a girl. But she was already married. How the hell did I get myself into this shit?

❧

"So are you going to buy something or did you just bring me here so I could get stuff?" Marya had asked me at CD Turf.

"Only if I really need something," I said. I didn't mention the fact that I was pretty broke. Most of my money was spent on cigarettes or at Josh's Pub.

Food wise, I usually only went to the Taco Bell close to where I was living. Probably because it was the cheapest in terms of food. I had tried White Castle but never really liked it too much.

And she had picked up close to ten cds. U2 imports that couldn't be found everywhere and some other stuff I wasn't too familiar with.

Never had heard of The Devlins. And she got a couple of things from Alanis Morrisette, that I wasn't too crazy about.

Hell, I didn't go there with her so I could shop. I went there so I could be with her. And no, I didn't make a move or anything along those lines.

I just wanted to be in her company. What good was that doing me? I can't explain but it just seemed so right.

"I am going outside for a smoke," I told her.

"Again?" she said.

"Well, I can't smoke with you in the car because you were freezing," I said.

"Whatever," she said.

So I went outside, sat on the curb, and lit a cigarette. It was really cold but I had my thick flannel shirt on and a woolen cap on my head.

"Always keep your head warm," my mother always told me. And that was one of her advices I always took. Maybe the only one.

"Shit" I said as the cigarette fell out of my hand and rolled away with the wind.

"Damn it," I thought as I pulled out another one and lit it.

Marya was definitely pretty. How could I possibly make her stay a little longer?

At least until she could see me the way I was starting to see her.

Chapter 44

"So the teachers never hit the kids?" I asked.

Joe and Lynn gave me a strange look that answered my question.

Yes, things were a lot different in the US. Somehow, wherever I went, I ended up feeling bad for the teachers. In my eyes, it was one of the most honorable professions around. In Pakistan, it was one of the lowest paid professions. So I felt bad for the teachers there because

they had been pretty close to poverty. At least at the school I had gone to... Islamabad College for Boys.

No, it wasn't a college like in the US. It was everything from kindergarten to fourteenth grade. Tenth grade was called Metric. Eleventh grade was referred to as "first year" and twelfth was "second year." I never stuck around to see what they had meant by those titles. Of course, then there was "third" and "fourth" year. It had been mixed up to fifth grade- mixed meaning co-educational. Boys and girls together. Then girls went to schools that were exclusively for girls and the boys stayed. Yes, they separated the boys and girls just around the time puberty hit, when hormones kicked in, and horniness took over. Yes, there were schools that were co-ed throughout but they were mostly private schools. There was no way that the government was going to support those dens of imminent sin.

But, the point I was getting at was that the teachers were very low paid. I saw kids, including myself, getting dropped off at school in cars while the teachers got there on foot.

The rich teachers had bicycles. Was it like that in every school? I don't know. I only went to my school. And that is why I felt bad for the teachers there. Because they were so poor. So, a lot of times, they would take their frustrations out on their students and it wasn't uncommon for students to get hit by teachers. A slap on the face was the easy one. Some teachers would make you put your hand out and then bring down a wooden ruler on your palms. Some teachers had rulers just for such occasions which they would cover with electrical tape to make the impact more forceful.

Or they could use the chalkboard erasers. But they were not the soft type of erasers that were used in American schools. They were about the same size but made of wood, with a soft material on the one side to erase the boards. And no, you didn't get hit by that side.

So the kids were disciplined there in that fashion.

I still felt bad for the teachers. The poor folks had to do something. I was, what you would consider, a troublemaker. So I got a lot of that disciplining there. And you know something? I never held it against any of those teachers. At the moment, I might have but when I thought of it later, I realized that I had deserved it.

In the US, I felt bad for the teachers because they had to take all the abuse from the students and all they could do was give them a bad grade or detention.

That is why American kids were so spoiled. Because of the inability of either parents or teachers to give them any sort of punishment that would have immediate consequences.

No, I was not advocating child abuse. But maybe, just maybe, there could be some way in between the two extremes that I saw. Thank God, I wasn't involved in making any such choices.

Oh, the kids were disciplined in Pakistan. You got a beating in school from the teachers. But you kept it to yourself. You didn't come home and tell the parents.

Because that could be a huge mistake. When your parents asked you how your day in school was, you'd better say fine. If you happened to mention anything about the punishments, then you'd better be prepared for another round. Now your dad was going to unleash his fury over why you had done something deserving punishment. He would know that the teachers didn't just go around dispensing slaps and beatings that were not justified. So dad would end up giving you a lashing for not being a good kid.

Why couldn't you just be a good boy and study like he had done when he was a kid? Did I have a horrible childhood full of abuse?

No. I would and could never say that. Looking back, I'd say that it taught me well and made me a better person. I wouldn't trade it for anything.

Chapter 45

I was having problems. Problems with everything. I couldn't sleep. I couldn't eat. I pretty much couldn't do anything. So all I did was smoke. One after another. Sometimes lit one from the cigarette that was almost done. A chain smoker, I think it was referred to. But that was all I could do.

I had been there before. Right after realizing what I felt for Marya Durani. And now it was a different Marya doing it to me. After Marya Durani, one thing I believed was good was that I could go to a bar and add some alcohol to my attempts at extinguishing my misery. Now I was in Pakistan. And there is no alcohol in Pakistan. Only the rubbing kind. I am sure there were plenty of places I could get some booze. But I just didn't know where to look. And in my new found misery, I just didn't feel like going out of my way.

The US was so much better. At least there were so many options right at your disposal whenever a time like this came. Or maybe I had just gotten too used to that system. Or I had been too out of touch with the Pakistani system.

"Yo, take a drag?" Mark had said to me many a times when I had been around and he had been smoking his joint.

"I'm good," I would always say refusing his offer.

"Yeah, too damn good," would be his reply.

I never got into pot, thank God. Cigarettes were enough for me.

"Remember when you had your first cigarette? How you got all light headed? Well imagine that feeling but a hundred times better," Mark had said countless times.

So I had taken a couple of drags off of a joint once. I swear to God that I hadn't really felt anything. But try telling that to those who had been around at the time. According to them, I had been totally "fucked up."

I didn't think so. Or could it be possible that I had been so messed up that I didn't recall. I liked to think that it wasn't so.

But whatever that feeling may have been, I wish I had it now. Or that buzz that came after a few drinks before you actually got drunk.

That moment when I had always stopped because that is all I had been looking for. Not to lose track of what was happening. Just a little happy feeling. A little bit of that which made me forget about my troubles for a while.

That is what I wish I had.

Because this was starting to hurt. How the hell did I always get myself into these positions?

I was always considered the nice guy. The "fag" who had a drunk chick all over him but didn't try anything because "it wouldn't be right."

I sometimes wish I wasn't the nice guy. Maybe Green Day had a point when they sang "Nice Guys Finish Last." If I wasn't last then why wasn't anybody behind me?

There I go again. Automatically classifying myself as a nice guy. A little vain, won't you say? But I honestly believed that I was a nice guy.

Not some conclusion that I had come to. And definitely not something that I would go around saying about myself. Yes, I know I did just say that about myself but this is different.

This is my confessional and I can say whatever I want. Whatever I can't say in real life is going to be said here. So I just praised myself. But I will also denounce myself. I already gave you reasons why I hated myself. Won't you agree with me and hate me for the same reasons I hated me?

I never told a lie. But once I got started, I couldn't stop.

I never got drunk but there were times when I felt the need to act like I was drunk.

“Are you okay, Irfan?” Marya Durani had asked me over the phone when I had called her a second time.

It was around midnight in New Jersey and I had just left Josh’s Pub. My intake had expanded. Now I had started drinking Coors Light. The draft was only a dollar and I realized that it was just as good since it got the job done while costing less.

But that wasn’t it. I would have three Coors Light drafts and then follow it up with a couple of Molson Ices. That got the job done.

So I had my fill when I had gotten on the phone and decided to call Marya in Pakistan. A little buzz didn’t stop me from being able to figure out that it must be around ten in the morning in Pakistan. The ten hour time difference put Pakistan ahead of the US. Probably the only thing it was ahead in.

“Yeah, I am fine,” I said even though there was a throbbing headache. Weren’t you supposed to get a hangover the morning after? Oh, well.

“What is it?” she asked. There was that little gap in the voice reaching my ear after leaving her mouth thousands of miles away.

I had really gotten lucky in the sense that she had been the one to pick up the phone. I only had around two dollars left on the calling card. That would hardly give me enough time. But it would give me enough time to say what I wanted to say.

“Mary,” I said, “I am sorry but I have no other way of saying this. I think I am in love with you. Actually I am pretty sure that I am in love with you. I know you are already engaged but I had no idea about it. I am sorry but I just don’t know what else to say.”

There was a moment of quiet. Then she spoke.

“I don’t know Irfan. The thing is that I really liked you, too. But my parents already have their mind set on me getting married to Amir. I didn’t pick him. They did and you know how things work here.”

“I am sorry,” I said feeling a little more light headed than I had a little while ago.

"Stop saying you are sorry. You didn't do anything. If anything, I should say I am sorry because I should have told you," she said.

And then the card finished. No warning about how much time was left. Just a click and then dead silence.

This time of night there wouldn't be any stores where I could get one.

"Shit, shit, shit," is all I could think as I put the phone back in its place.

When I thought about it later on, I realized how unlike me that episode had just been. I mean, when all was to be taken into consideration, I had to look at it the same way I would look at a movie. If what had just occurred was in a movie, I would probably roll my eyes at how cheesy it was. Because that is what I had just done. Something so cheesy that I wouldn't be the only who would roll their eyes. Critics would shun the movie for being too overly romantic and clichéd.

But that is what I had come down to. To being a cliché. A hackneyed character in the dramatics of life.

It might as well start raining so I could do my "crying in the rain." But it would not rain. It was pretty damn cold. If anything it would snow. But it was too cold to snow.

Which reminded me of the many arguments I had with people.

"What do you mean its too cold to snow?" they would ask me if I suggested it was too cold to snow.

"What about the North Pole?"

"Well," I would try to explain, "it doesn't snow in Antarctica. Its just so cold there that everything has been frozen solid. That is why the world's largest desert is Antarctica."

This was followed by looks of amazement by many. I, of course, was right. When you said desert, people pictured sand and dunes. Probably with Arabs riding camels.

But the true definition of a desert was any place with precipitation that was below a certain amount. I don't know how much that amount was but I did know that by precipitation, it meant rain. And it didn't rain there. But try explaining that to people who had their own images of a desert etched in their minds.

And once again, I digress. Its easy to do when you are dealing with a chapter of your life that you wish hadn't been.

So there I was, sitting on the floor of my apartment. Yes, it was cold inside my apartment since I never turned the heat too high. I liked it cold. There was just something about bundling up in a nice thick quilt, that the heat from the vents didn't do... I had been home all day and decided to use my home phone to make this call.

That was a good choice, I had realized, since it gave me more space. You never knew when somebody else might come to use the payphone you were on. They wouldn't tell you to get off. Or just stand there and give you a hard look that said their call was more important than yours.

Chapter 46

I was hanging out at the Kinnsville Public Library, like I often did when I had nothing else to do. I checked out some magazines, browsed the newspapers, and then decided to browse through the books. For some odd reason, I decided to see if they had a book which I hadn't even thought of for a long time. I went to the R section and started going through the authors there. And I couldn't believe it when I actually saw the name I never thought I would see. Salman Rushdie.

The guy had written a few books but the one that they had there was the one I never thought I would ever see. The Satanic Verses. But why should I have been shocked? This was America.

And all I could think of was, when one of my favorite hangouts in Pakistan came under attack.

That place was the American Center in Islamabad. That was one of the two places where my parents would drop me off at when I didn't have school. The other place was the British Council Library. I had gotten membership at both places and loved the nice tranquil environment there. I spent many hours at the library and the center. Which could be one reason why I didn't have too much problem with the English language when I came to the US. My parents wanted me to look at all the educational stuff. But I had other things on my mind. I would always be where the fiction was. Life was enough reality for me.

And that is why I preferred the British Council Library. Because they had a lot more fiction there. The American Center was mostly dry, educational stuff.

And then I stumbled across something that changed my whole outlook of the place. They also had books about the cinema... and non-fiction that I could get into. I started spending hours going through those books, reading about movies, and checking out the reviews.

And, I was shocked when I came across some pretty racy photographs in those books. Last Tango in Paris was a definitely a movie I had to check out if I could ever manage to.... It doesn't make sense that a Muslim country would allow those kinds of books in such a public place.

But these were encyclopedias. A sub-genre was the cinema. And nobody probably ever thought of going through the place's inventory in such detail.

So that is all I did. Read about movies, browsed the fiction, and picked up something educational when I knew it was nearing the time my father would come to pick me up. And I also made secret lists where I wrote down names of movies that I definitely had to see when I could.

The Godfather, Rocky, Raging Bull, Midnight Cowboy.

One day I would see them.

And then in 1988, Rushdie's **Satanic Verses** was published. There were protests all everywhere around the globe over its blasphemous content.

The protestors in Pakistan decided to go after the American Center in Islamabad, the country's capital. What started out as a peaceful protest, turned violent when the American Center was reached. They threw rocks, bottles, and whatever was available at the building. They even attacked the security guards outside the building. The guards were Pakistanis but their crime was standing guard in front of a building that housed something that was insulting to their religion.

But, no, the book wasn't there. It was just the notion that Rushdie had gotten it published in the US. Actually, I don't even know it his publisher was in the US. I don't even know why they chose America as their scapegoat since Rushdie wasn't even American.

But the American Center prevailed and after a while things cooled down. Rushdie was forgotten as the Muslim community probably found something else to denounce. My parents, though, didn't want me going to that place again because you never knew when things would change to ease some mullah's boredom.

One thing I couldn't figure out was how the British Council Library withstood those furious times. After all, Rushdie was British.

Who knows?

But getting back to the time I stumbled across the **Satanic Verses** in the Kinnsville Public Library.

Of course, I had to take it out so I could read it and see with my own eyes the text that had caused all those troubles I had seen in person.

I took it home and started reading the book. After going through a few chapters, I realized that the book was heinous. Heinously boring, that is. How could they have been so enraged by such a boring piece of crap? Nothing was directly offensive but if you dug into the symbolic significance of the characters, then maybe there was something to it. But I thought it was still a piece of crap not worthy of the attention that had been brought to it.

I never finished it since in my eyes, it sucked. So I went back and took out **It** by Stephen King. Now that was a good book.

But then I had been a fan of King ever since I read Cujo at the tender age of eight. So I wasn't normal. But I read it all the way through even though I had to keep turning to a dictionary. And that was another problem.

A lot of the cuss words, which I didn't know at the time, were not in the dictionary I was using. What kind of dictionary could that be?

Well Pakistan and India used to be under British rule like most of the world in the old days. The Brits left but their influence remained. Which is why my dictionary wasn't a Webster's. It was The Pocket Oxford Dictionary though the pocket had to be huge to carry that miniature mammoth.

So a lot of the words that King used were not in that dictionary. But I got the point.

Big dog good but big dog with rabies very bad. So the book didn't really terrify me but it did turn me onto King's world. And that was another problem I had with The American Center. They had Faulkner, Hawthorne, and other literary types. But they didn't have King, Ludlum, or any others that were my type. So I was actually coaxed into turning to books about movies. Not my fault.

Chapter 47

I had no idea how taya ji could do this with such devotion. He had to be devoted since he had been doing this most of his life. I had been doing this for a couple of weeks and was already getting sick of it. The same people. The same bullshit. The same questions. What does this bill say? What does my son say? Did my son have any more kids? Boy? Girl? When is he coming back? He didn't marry some girl over there?

The same bull. Then I realized what this was making me and I didn't like it. I found another reason to hate myself.

These were simple people and these were their lives. How dare I look at their life as being any less than what mine was?

So I just kept smiling, smoking, and doing what my great taya ji had dedicated his life to... Many considered, what he was doing, below them. They would never stoop to doing something like that if they had the education. So they wouldn't have some high paying job but whatever they could manage to land would be better than this type of thing. Because that is all they could see it as... a type of thing. Not a real profession.

His people shouldn't have him easing their self-inflicted handicaps. They had a choice. They could get an education and learn to read and learn to write.

As if getting an education was so easy in Pakistan. Unfortunately, even that was a luxury. To get your child into a school required having some connections.

If you didn't know somebody, your child would probably end up in some school where the teachers were on the same educational level as the students. Government schools were hard to get into so you could send your kid to some private school. And there were plenty of those. No special certification was needed. If there was, then there wasn't anything a little bribe couldn't handle. So there were so many private schools that people had opened in their houses. A little modification and your house became a school. It was just something that could probably never be fathomed by an American.

Which is why I was extremely grateful for being born in Pakistan. The Lord made it possible for me to see the bad along with the good.

But this letter writing was definitely bad for my health. Because there wasn't too much to be read or written. So I just sat there and smoked. One after another.

Went through a couple of packs easily. Oh, I didn't just smoke. I smoked, I thought, and I hoped. I thought of the Marya that I had lost and hoped to see the Marya that I had found.

Once again, it happened. What I had started to believe that if you hoped for something strong enough, it can happen. Sure, if that was so true then why was I so damn miserable?

I guess it can't work every time since, I am sure, the good Lord has some reason behind the way things happen. But whatever. The point is that it happened. I wanted Marya to come with some letter to read, and she did.

I have no idea how many cigarettes I had had when she came to my table. She is going to save me, I thought to myself.

Get over it, I realized. She is not saving you. She just wants a letter read and doesn't give a damn about you smoking yourself to death. That was probably a lot truer than my wishful thinking.

"Hello," she said taking a seat across me. Actually the only seat across from me.

"How are you?" I replied trying not to telegraph what my heart was feeling.

Pure joy. Why couldn't all the people coming to be like her? … Because then I would stop

appreciating what I was getting. Yeah, that's it.

"I am okay," she said putting her beaten-down pocket book on the table and opening it. "I got another letter for you to read, if you don't mind."

'Honey, if I minded I wouldn't be sitting out here freezing my ass off.' I just thought that and didn't really say it, of course.

"No, no, not a problem," I said reaching for the letter.

Yes, it was from her husband, a man I had never met, didn't care to meet, and had started to hate. Yes, I hated the guy.

Because of what he had and what he had left behind in search of money. I wasn't really thinking straight, was I? Because I am sure he wouldn't be doing what he was doing if he had a choice. He wouldn't leave his beautiful wife to go in search of money. I actually felt bad for him.

So in this small period of time, my mind had pretty much surfed the entire spectrum of human emotion. There was the joy of seeing her. The misery of knowing that I didn't have her.

The hatred for the one who did have her. The compassion to understand why he wasn't with her. The urge to turn that to my favor. The self loathing upon realizing what I was thinking.

And finally, the acceptance of the reality that I wanted to do so.

Yes, I was an asshole because I was going to lie.

Chapter 48

Bad was the song that had gotten me into U2. I can't really recall where I heard it but it was just such a beautiful song. And I had no idea that it was titled **Bad**. That was one of the things Marya Durani had helped me with. I was a U2 fan though I wasn't as rabidly into their music as I wound up getting into.

"What's that one song where he's going 'I am not sleeping'?" I had asked her hoping she could help me since she was a huge fan. After all, she had come all the way to the US to see them play.

Then I had started to hum the tune, hoping I wasn't coming across as some *doofus.*

"Oh, that's **Bad**," she said immediately. "The title, I mean. Its on The Unforgettable Fire."

"Good. Thank you," I said. "I definitely have to get that because that thing is so stuck in my head."

"Oh, its a great cd but then I say that about anything from U2," she said.

Once again, we were sitting at the diner. She had a cup of black coffee while I was sitting there with a slice of chocolate cheese cake. Shazia had something or other to do and had just told us to go ahead without her. I had taken Marya to Macy's where she had picked up some kids clothes for her nieces or nephews. Honestly, I didn't give a crap who they were, for it was buying me some time. Time that I could be with her.

After the stop at Macy's, I had suggested stopping off at some diner for a cup of coffee or something. She agreed and we just stopped in at one of the diners populating Route 22. I can't even remember the name of the place because, once again, I didn't give a crap as long as it bought me some time with her. So we stopped in for coffee or something.

She got the coffee, I got the something, and we talked about whatever came to mind.

"So how are things in Pakistan these days?" I said.

"Well you remember how they were bad when you left? Now they are a lot worse," she said. "Everything is just so damn expensive. And the people don't make shit. And it is so crowded. So many people. I mean, it would be okay if they were halfway civilized. But, no, they act like such animals. There is filth all over the place. And don't even talk about the traffic."

Oh, yeah, she loved it there. We talked about things there and things in the US. Then we talked about movies and music. She didn't like Pakistani movies and felt the same about Indian movies. She just watched English language films, American or British, when she got the chance.

And, of course, she didn't like Pakistani or Indian music either.

Well, her dedication to U2 should have told me that much.

So here was a girl that seemed perfect for me. She was pretty and it can be said that part appealed to my shallower side. And she was into the kind of music I was into. Hell, she told me the title of the song that had been haunting me for so long. I had actually ended up going to music stores where I would ask the clerks if they knew what song it was. I was the nut humming to the people in hopes of some recognition. Nobody knew shit. The store workers just knew whatever was popular at the time and it didn't matter if their knowledge was going to be worthless in a few months. All I knew was that the artist was U2 and that wasn't much help since they had such a vast catalogue. If anything, the people I dealt with would know stuff off of their newest cd, **Pop**.

Thank God I met Marya. If anything, she was able to put my musically inquisitive side at peace. **Bad.**

Who, in a million years, could have guessed that such an epically beautiful song would have such a simple and brief title?

But music aside, she was Pakistani. So my parents would be happy.

This was just too perfect. Oh, but I already told you where this would end up. Totally sucked, to put it in terms that my American buddies could relate to.

Yes, it not only sucked, but hurt like hell. Crippled me. But maybe there was a greater purpose. Was I justifying it for myself the way my elders had justified their theological faith and beliefs? So us humans aren't that different after all is taken apart. We believe, we are shattered, and we hope for a better outcome than the one that shook us. All I could think of when I looked past my phase of denial was that I, along with the rest of the human race, was so fucked.

❦

Sorry about dropping the F bomb but no other word seems to capture the feeling that was there.

Chapter 49

"Once again, I have to ask you how you want me to do it? Do you want me to read it to you or do you want me to read the entire thing and tell you what it says?" I asked Marya as she started to look like she was having second thoughts about me doing this.

"Well..." she started to say and then stopped. Then she started to think. How did she want some guy who was probably around her age to do it. She wasn't dealing with taya ji, any more. I guess it was different with the old timer. It had to be since Pakistan was a whole different world when it came to treating people who were older than you. It made me think of how different things were in the US. How everybody was treated pretty much the same regardless of their age. It was good in the sense that you were pretty casual with everyone. There were no formalities of treating everybody you ran into differently. You didn't have to respect somebody just because they were older. The respect was distributed to the one's who deserved it. And in the same sense, it was bad because everybody was treated like a peer. In my eyes, there should have been a little more respect given to people because they were older. At least start off with a respectful tone. Then you could change your behavior according to what seemed appropriate. It wasn't good to just start off like you were talking to a kid when the person being dealt with was quite older than you.

"I guess you can just tell me what he says," she finally said, after a long moment of thought.

"Okay," I said as I started reading the letter to myself. The guy had nice handwriting, at least. The letter was written in Urdu, of course, the native language of Pakistan -spoken like Hindi but written like Arabic. Right to left. It had been one of my showing off bits in the USA. Showing people how their name would be written in my language.

People, especially girls, would be really impressed when I wrote their name in Urdu. And then, of course, people would ask me about profanity in Urdu. How to say this and how to say that, which is one thing I had learned over the years, whenever somebody learned something in a different language, the profanity came first. I, myself, could curse in English, Urdu, Spanish, Portuguese, Italian, Mandarin, Polish, and God knows how many other languages.

Basically what Marya's husband had written was the same crap he had written the last time. How he was working so hard, making a little money, living like a peasant, and restless to get back to Pakistan. And that's what bothered me. He was restless to get back to Pakistan but didn't mention anything about coming back to her. What an asshole.

"He says that he is working two jobs and has managed to save some money. Not a lot since his roommate left and he is paying all the rent for the last couple of months," I started. And then I thought I should add something to it. "He says that he misses you very much and can't wait to get back to you."

She smiled. And then I started to get a little cheesy. "He misses your smile and can't believe he had to leave your beautiful presence to make some more money. He hates being away from you and can't wait to get back to you so," I hesitated, "you two can start a family." She was starting to blush since, once again, this was Pakistan and these types of things were not said to the females. At least not by some guy you were not married to.

"And that is about all," I said realizing I was out of ideas.

"Thank you," she said getting up. "I don't have any money with me but I will bring some the next time. I am going to visit my parents and will ask them for some since its not that easy without him around. Your taya let me pay him once a month."

"Its okay," I said. "He told me and you can pay whenever you can."

"Thank you," she said again as she started to turn away.

"Its alright, " I said as she started walking away. Yes, thank you for coming, I thought.

Thank you for making me want to go on.

Chapter 50

Time to go back to my days in the USA.

"You know what you need?" Jeff said as I gave him back his change.

"No," I replied. "And you know what, I don't give a crap about what you think I need."

"You need a chick," he went on ignoring what I had said. "Unless you are not into that type of thing. I mean, if you like guys, that is fine. More power to you. But you need a chick. Or a dude."

I couldn't really get over the fact that Jeff was having this kind of conversation with me. He was pretty old. Maybe late sixties. Fat, bald, and with a habit of smoking three packs a day. And not three packs of the wussy kind of stuff that people like me and others smoked. He was a Camel smoker. The real Camels. The short ones with no filters on them.

And from what he had told me, he had been smoking since he was twelve, an age when I didn't even know how to use a lighter.

That had convinced me that smoking wasn't really that lethal. Sure, it wasn't the healthiest of habits but I had known a few people who didn't even get second hand smoke, ate healthy, exercised regularly, and still dropped dead from a heart attack or something.

And according to Jeff, his brand of smokes was a lot better than all this "light and ultra-light shit" because who knew the kind of junk they were adding to make up for what they were taking out. I didn't argue with him. Maybe the old timer had point. A point I wasn't keen on debating. Actually a point that I didn't care to worry about. Whatever happens, happens. If health wasn't the killer then there was always that unexpected car wreck that could ruin your plans. Yes, I was that optimistic.

"No, I don't like guys and I don't think I want to commit to some woman," I said.

Sure my lack of having a girlfriend had started rumors about my sexuality but I never cared to pay it too much attention. They could think whatever they wanted. I really didn't care.

"Come on Irf, you are getting old. Now is the time," he persisted. "Oh, I know, you probably got some woman already picked out by your mommy and daddy. Some Pakistanian broad. Am I right?"

"First of all, its Pakistani and not Pakistanian. Second, I am not going for that arranged marriage shit. I know that and my parents know that."

Thank God, a couple of guys walked in and asked me for some cigarettes. That deterred Jeff for a while and bought me some time. He was one of these old timers I had gotten friendly with while working for the Patels. He was part of my elder friends that I had managed to make while working there.

And according to him, I should be "banging" some broad on a regular basis. Once again, I couldn't get over the kind of thinking that these old people possessed.

Well, I guess they were just able to say it here unlike the old people in Pakistan who probably held it in.

The guys left and Jeff stood there by the papers shaking his head.

"Seriously, I hate to see a young fellow like you miss out on all the fun. I wish I was your age. I mean, look at these chicks walking around. They are asking for it."

"Well," I said, "some of these girls you are talking about could be your granddaughters, you dirty old man."

He just huffed, shook his head, and walked out the door. Thank God, I thought.

But maybe he had a point.

It wouldn't come across as being to manly if I say that I was a little lonely. But, I don't give a damn, because you don't know me in person. This is my confessional and I think I have already said stuff that I should be more ashamed of than this little factoid. Let me see now, I was nineteen at the time and didn't have a significant other. Hell, I didn't even have an insignificant other. Had never gotten into that side of life because, frankly, I was still trying to figure out my place in this world, and trying to meet my parents' expectations. But I already told you that those expectations didn't really get a shot at being met. I gave up on going to college, started living in my own little apartment, got a little job at that convenience store, and observed life happening around me while trying to get a grip of what's going on. Almost like trying to hop onto a carousel that had started going around without me. So it wouldn't be a shock if I said that the most relatable song for me was Loser from Beck. Because that is how I felt. Like a God damn loser.

And it was these feelings of dank hopelessness that had led me to Josh's Pub.

Had I become an alcoholic? I wouldn't say that, even though, I was there every night. But not to get hammered. Just to get that little buzz going. That feeling of artificial happiness.

And I already told you that it is where I fell head over heals in love with my first Marya.

Chapter 51

I was a late bloomer. Why? Because I started smoking when I was seventeen. Graduating high school made me start, because I was so damn jittery about going into the real world. Supposedly that is what was awaiting me outside high school. So I started smoking.

It was more for health reasons than anything. It was the only thing that would keep me from losing my mind. I checked out all the bad habits around and decided to go with smoking. It was awesome. I felt I was meant to smoke ever since I got that high of my first cigarette.

And the rest is history. At least, my history.

The biggest pain was trying to get the cigarettes. I was seventeen and the Surgeon General, in all his wisdom, had narrowed the safe age for smoking down to eighteen years. I looked mature enough but every now and then, there would be that extra dedicated, ass-kisser of a store clerk who would ask for an ID. But, I managed.

In Pakistan there was no such thing as a legal age. I had seen kids around nine or ten years old, smoking. That was back when I lived in Pakistan. Now that I was back and spending a lot of time at the train station, I saw even more children smoking. Yes, children. Not kids. Because, in my opinion, there is a certain degree of maturity that makes you a kid. So a child falls before that phase. And these were children smoking. Ones you wouldn't want playing with fire. But they were also poor children. Poverty was rampant and these children were doing stuff that would have been against all child welfare laws in the US. Picking up heavy luggage for the passengers getting on or off the trains. All for a few rupees. So they could buy some food for themselves and their families. And, of course, buy themselves some cigarettes.

Was smoking a status symbol of sorts? I guess so because not many in the middle class smoked. Either the lower class smoked or the rich people smoked. Strange but that is what I had observed.

❧

"Here's another one from my bum son," the old lady said throwing a letter on the table.

"Okay," I said reaching for the crumpled envelope and realizing all the love this woman had for her son.

It was Masi Zainab. Masi wasn't her first name. Just a prefix like Mr. or Mrs., except that it wasn't really a prefix you sought because it pretty much described you as an old lady. So I didn't call her Masi to her face. But when I would tell taya ji about whom I had dealt with, I would call her Masi.

Anyway, her son was in Dubai, United Arab Emirates. A lot of Pakistanis were there. Mostly the laborer types, I think.

I read the letter and started to tell her what he had written. The same old stuff that everyone else seemed to write. How they are working so hard, saving money, and restless without their loved ones. And that is what her son had written. But there was a little twist at the end. He had gotten in touch with someone who had a business in London and the guy was offering him a job there. So he was going to England in a couple of weeks and not returning to Pakistan as he had told her before.

Should I tell her or not? I decided that my lies were getting a little too rampant. And it wasn't like this was bad news.

So I told her and it turned out it was terrible news.

"But his fiancée's family is already pushing me to tell him to come back and marry her," she said in a voice teetering on sobbing.

"I don't know," I said. And, frankly, I didn't. I was just supposed to read the letters, not offer counseling.

She put her elbows on the table, put her face in her hands, and started sobbing and cursing her son in a very loud voice.

People started giving us looks that were basically sympathizing with the old lady and shunning me for what I had done.

And what was it that I had done? I had no idea and knew even less about what to do.

Then she got up and started walking away, still sobbing.

Thank God, I thought pulling out my cigarettes and lighting one up. Then I realized that she didn't pay me. Whatever.

I wasn't about to go after her for my payment. The hell with it, I thought as I leaned back in my chair.

It was then that I realized I was getting to be what I didn't want to be. I was starting to become judgmental. One thing I had learned in the US was not to judge people.

It wasn't something that I was taught in school. I just happened to have made friends in all walks of life. And one friend had pointed out that I was extremely judgmental.

"So you are saying I am nuts?" I said to her. "Judge… mental?"

She laughed and said that I was twisting her words around.

"No… Judgmental… One word," Berry had said as we were sitting in the Ridgewood High School library.

Yes, she was one of my girl friends. Not a girlfriend; separate the two words. A friend I had made who happened to be of the opposite sex.

She wasn't that much older than me. I was in tenth grade and fifteen years old at the time. She was a senior and eighteen. About to graduate and, man, I missed her already. She was going to some college in Michigan. That was another thing I didn't get… Everyone wanted to graduate and go to some college out of state. I guess get away from their parents.

I think it would have been better to stick around a little longer. Hold on to your innocence a little longer.

"I mean, you just go ahead and judge people without even trying to see what they might see," she continued. She was only three years older than me but talking like she was a grandma or something.

"Have a little empathy. Or you don't know what the fuck that means?"

She used the F word which meant she was getting ticked off at me. I didn't want that.

"What do you mean?" I said, realizing I was putting my guard down.

"I mean that you just look at that girl, see all that make up, and label her a slut. You don't know her background. You don't know the kind of home she is coming from. Maybe putting some lipstick and eye liner on makes her feel a little more confident. It doesn't mean she is ready to put out. She may be a lot harder to get to than some of these girls walking around with their eyes always looking down. Maybe mom and dad are a couple of tight wads who never let her do anything fun. And this is her time to be a little free. That's what I mean," she said looking me straight in the eyes and frowning at the smile that was starting to appear on my face.

"Okay, grandma," I said with my smile getting broader.

"Whatever," she said, "you don't give a shit."

But I did give a shit. I was extremely willing to learn. I didn't limit my learning to teachers, books, and blackboards. Everything was a teacher.

And Berry may not have blown my mind but she did manage to make a dent. I kept thinking of what she said.

Since that day, I don't think I ever saw anyone as being what appeared before me. I always tried to look past what was and tried to see what might have been.

But how the hell did I lose that side when sitting there reading this old lady's letter? Why had I just jumped to this conclusion of labeling her a shallow and misunderstanding mother who couldn't just let her son be? I didn't know if she had any other kids. Maybe this was her only son and all her dreams were attached to him. Which was still a little unfair for him to be put in such a situation where all he did, had to please those that brought him into this world. Maybe empathy was the reason I was so screwed up. Maybe it was just easier to just sit back and judge.

But it was too late for me. The E word was too far embedded in my mind to be excavated.

I had no choice in the matter anymore. I just had to relate to everyone before coming to a final decision.

Empathy sucked.

Chapter 52

"Did I ask too much? More than a lot? You gave me nothing. Now its all I've got."

My words. My song.

One from U2.

Of all the Ones out there, this is the one that became mine.

I mean, One is a pretty popular song title. Metallica has a song titled One. Elton John has one. Even the Bee Gees did a song titled One. Okay, Elton John's song is titled The One and not just One. But my point is that its a pretty popular song title, won't you say? There may be many more songs with that title. Who knows. Maybe because one is the loneliest number.

Actually, now that I think about it, I believe that Three Dog Night also had a song with that title. I am pretty sure. But I refuse to look things up. Especially in the music department. I know music. I like to think that I do. So all my musical knowledge is what I have gotten to know from just living a music-enriched existence.

But One from U2 is my song. Maybe its because of that previous line. Actually its probably because of that line.

A song I would like to dedicate to Marya Durani. Because she gave me nothing. Just something that came to me to tempt me… to make me want her. That siren. That bitch.

I can't believe I just used the B word to describe her.

It wasn't her fault. She didn't really tempt me. But she did lead me on. She didn't tell me the truth when she knew I had tripped and was going to fall.

Yes, that bitch.

I never got into U2 as much as I did after we met. It was synchronicity. It was meant to be. The United States was a huge country. Why would she come to see U2 in Miami but then decide to stop by New Jersey? They were far apart. Why? Because she was meant to meet me at Josh's Pub.

That is how I justified it for myself.

I was a U2 fan. So, obviously, we were meant to be. But I pissed off a lot of U2 fans, including her, when I spoke of the band.

"The Joshua Tree is okay," I would say and be met with disbelief from those who had followed the band and considered that to be probably the best album of all time. "I think Achtung Baby is a lot better. Probably their best."

Now people would just be pissed off by this time. I didn't know shit, they would say. I didn't care. For me, Achtung Baby was the best album of all time. And that is before I met her. That is before she made One mine.

Yes, did I ask too much? I don't think I asked anything.

For the kids at Ridgewood High, Metallica's One was the one. A Bunch of head bangers. Actually, there were groups. One group was into heavy stuff.

The other group was into rap. And by rap, I mean stuff that was passing for rap in those days... MC Hammer... Vanilla Ice... People who wouldn't have any longevity, in my opinion.

Then there were the head bangers... Winger, Motley Crue, and Warrant fans... I didn't get into that either. But I liked the tee shirts that they had. So I was a little morbid but I liked the clothing with skulls and stuff on it. I even got myself a Metallica tee shirt with two skulls staring at each other... Sad but True written on the back. Not because I was into that music. Just because I thought it looked cool. The morbid mentality that I had.

But I had always done my own thing. I was never into what passed for "hip" at the time. I was into The Smiths, The Cure, and even The Rolling Stones.

Of course, the song that got my morbid personality into that last one was Paint It Black.

But nobody around me cared for those *old geezers*. And like Metallica was going to stay young forever.

My mother would have killed me if she saw me wearing that Metallica tee shirt. Not because she wasn't a fan but because of the skulls on it. Munhoos is what she would call it. A bad omen. Something that seeps into real life if you flaunt it the way I supposedly was. But for me it was just a tee shirt with a cool picture on it. Even my aunt didn't take too kindly to it.

"Where did you get that piece of junk?" she asked me the first day I stepped into the living room on my way out the door. "They let people wear that in school?"

"Yes, why not? Its just a band name and picture from their album," I said knowing fully well that this picture was not on the cover of Metallica's cd. But my aunt didn't know that. There was no way she would know that and even if she did know that, it wouldn't make a difference.

"Come on, aunty, its just a tee shirt," I said as I stepped out the door.

All I heard was her giving a loud sigh and saying something about how my parents would be so disappointed if they saw me dressed like that.

My parents didn't care. At least I thought that they wouldn't care as long as my report card was good.

But I am digressing, aren't I? I have no idea why I just flash backed to my high school days.

What I should be talking about is that siren named Marya Durani.

I had around fifty or so cds. When I would leave for Pakistan, I would only have around ten or so. Why?

Because I did something I never thought I could. I sold a lot of them. Not because I needed money. But because I was a moron.

I knew that a lot of stuff I had, Marya had as well. So I went to CD Turf and sold a lot of stuff that we both had. Because her and I were meant to be together. And we wouldn't need two copies of the same cd. So out went the stuff from Oasis, Blur, and Del Amitri to name a few.

Like I said, I was a moron. At least I had the sense to hold onto U2. For the moment, our supposed couple had two copies of most of the U2 catalog.

There were two Joshua Trees, two Achtung Babies, two Pops, two Rattle and Hums, two Zooropas, and two Unforgettable Fires. I held on to those because I needed them until Marya and I could be together. I thought of dumping Limp Bizkit because she didn't like them. But I figured that I had to have something that was just mine. Like she had her Alanis Morrisette and Tori Amos. I had my Limp Bizkit and Eve 6. Yes, I was a dreamer. Or a damn moron.

Chapter 53

It wasn't too easy… Life, that is. Or maybe it was my fault. Maybe I was the one making it difficult for myself.

It could have been simple. It could have been good. But I didn't know that. All I knew was that I had this irresistible urge to do things differently. It would have been so easy if I had just studied in the US, became a doctor, started a practice, or gone back to Pakistan and started there. I could have made a lot of money since an American educated doctor in Pakistan would have been huge in Pakistan.

But I never wanted to be a doctor. Yes, I always said I was going to be a doctor when people asked me what I wanted to do when I grew up. But I just said that because that was all I had been told. That's what my parents had raised me as wanting. Everybody in Pakistan wanted their kid to be a doctor. Which is when I started to question that country's future.

How far could a nation full of doctors go? And most of these people were sending their kids abroad to study medicine. How many of these kids were actually going to come back to Pakistan and start their practice. Not too many, I thought. Not after they had gotten a taste of the good life beyond that country's borders. Sure there would be the few with their noble cause of serving their motherland. But they would be few. Very few.

Apparently, there were only two career options for me. Two worthy ones, anyway. I could be a lawyer or I could be a doctor. Being a lawyer wasn't such a prime option because I wasn't that sharp. That's what I was told pretty bluntly by my family.

Yes, I was smart but to be a lawyer you had to have a certain degree of confidence that I didn't possess. That is what I was told and I didn't argue. Guess that alone made the point.

So I was on my way to becoming a doctor. Not that I wanted to. I realized that it wasn't such a smart choice when some friends and I went bowling one night.

Bill worked at some delicatessen and had a little mishap while cutting a role. He put a pretty deep gash on his index finger. He bandaged it up and figured it was all good. But then the genius decided to go bowling that same night. The bandage came off and blood started flowing. So we decided to take him to the nearest emergency room since the blood wasn't showing any signs of stopping. So there we were at the emergency room and the doctor started to stitch up his finger. I was there and Bill's girlfriend, Amanda, was there. She was fine but I started to get a little light headed and nauseous when I saw the doctor go about his needlework. So much so that I had to be given a chair so that I could rest.

Me as a doctor? After that night, those plans started to seem a little unrealistic. Yes, being a doctor definitely went out as a career option for me since I was such a "pussy."

I figured that I would just hover around until something appealing enough came along.

It never did.

Maybe the elders in Pakistan were right when they said that people should concentrate on building a career first. Once that is all done, then turn the attention to getting a mate, and starting a family. The only thing that bothered me was that I was willing to go along with that.

That is why I never had a girlfriend. Because I was respecting my parents' expectations in doing things in the right order the Pakistani way.

It wasn't my fault that I fell for someone. I swear to God, I had not planned it. But then these things can never be planned, can they?

All I did know was that I could have never been a doctor or lawyer. I just wasn't the type.

One thing that had always bothered me about myself was how much I disliked being around… I almost said that I hated being around but decided that hate was too extreme. Anyway, what I meant by that was that I just didn't seem to fit.

I wasn't made to be here. I took everything too hard. I couldn't really live my life to the fullest because there was always something bothering me.

Want an example?

Okay, I will give you a few.

Pakistan was tough because I felt the unfairness of life was magnified there. At least that is what I thought when I saw life in the US. But even before I had set foot in the US, I felt that way. There were too much poverty there. I saw old ladies going through trash, finding something edible, proceeding to sit there on the side of the road and eating it like it was the best meal they ever had. Maybe it was the best thing they had in a long time. And all this went on when people sat at nearby hotels and ate their fancy foods in clear view of the paupers.

Sometimes it wasn't old ladies. Sometimes it was little kids in tattered clothes being dragged by their parents, slowing down because they saw something in the pile of trash they had just passed. Sometimes my parents would take me out to have some ice cream. I never liked eating at the eateries or ice cream parlors because then the beggars could see me eating something that they couldn't even dream of ever having... it just wasn't fair. Which is why I hated it when someone complained about something being unfair and being met with "life's not fair" as a response.

Yes, life wasn't fair. But I believed that it was my God given duty to be as fair as I possibly could be to my fellow man.

Yes, I was a pussy.

One thing that bothered me even more was when I realized that I couldn't bear to see the hurt that beliefs caused. What do I mean? My mother was very religious. Always kept her head covered, prayed five times a day, and did whatever else Islam demanded of her. My father was not religious at all even though he made sure I was raised with all the traditional Muslim values.

What hurt my mother was when The Satanic Verses from Salman Rushdie came out. She never read it. But it was talked about enough so that she knew it was a book that was insulting to her religion.

She actually cried because she didn't understand why someone would say such bad things about her beliefs. She didn't push her beliefs on anyone and didn't falsify anybody's beliefs. She believed what she believed because that is what she had been taught. And I just didn't like it that my mother's faith had been trivialized.

That is how I was.

Chapter 54

Marya Durani ruined me. She wasn't that pebble that caused a ripple in my tranquil existence. She was a boulder that caused an unprecedented upheaval. She made me realize what was missing. Something I never thought about before.

I wasn't lonely until I met her. After her, I knew that there was something missing. Something lacking that was never suspected of being absent. I didn't need anybody. I was fine. Then that sudden aching that made me want her to be there. That aching that made me want her to be there to fill that void I had apparently been ignoring. Until then it was just that empty feeling that overcame me when I didn't have anything else to do. Then it became amplified. I wanted her to be there with me. I pinpointed it as being an indication of loneliness.

How could I be lonely? I was fine on my own. I didn't need anybody to be in my way.

In my way to what? Then I realized I was going nowhere. I had no real purpose. I was just wandering through life. I was a damn waste of space. I just worked at the little store, hung out in a bar, watched movies, bull-shitted with people. If I was gone tomorrow, there would only be some space left vacant. My friends would miss me for a few days and then move on. My parents would miss me. But not because of something I had done or achieved. They would only miss me because I was their son. I was nothing. I had done shit. I had achieved shit. I had only done nothing.

ॐ

I wanted to matter.

I wanted to make an impression by accomplishing something.

I wanted to be loved for being me and not just by people who had to love me.

I wanted to be loved by someone who had gotten to know me and found something there that was worthy of their love. I was a wreck. Was this what being in love was like? If it was then I wasn't really too crazy about this emotion that had seemed to have overtaken everything I had read, heard, or seen.

As I said, I had a pretty encyclopedic knowledge of music. Even if I wasn't into the type of music, I knew something about it. But at that moment, I drew a blank. I knew there was a song about what I was going through. But I couldn't even recall the title of the song. All I knew was that the chorus was about my predicament.

"I didn't know I was looking for love until I found you." Yes, that was the chorus. Maybe it was also the title. Not the entire thing. Just, "I didn't know I was looking for love." Something like that. Like I said, I was drawing a blank. But my knowledge of music got me a lot of attention from girls. They would come to me and hum a tune because they wanted to attach an artist and title to what was stuck in their head.

It all started when I was sitting in the Ridgewood High School Library and browsing some magazines.

Two girls at a nearby table were talking.

"I just can't get that friggin' song out of my head. I don't even remember where I heard it."

That got my attention.

"How does it go?" I asked the one who was talking.

She turned around and gave me a strange look, then said, "Excuse Me?"

"I am sorry, I just heard you two talking about some song you were having trouble with. I was just wondering if I could help you out," I said.

They both gave me that strange look. They didn't know me. And from my looks, they were highly doubtful about my ability to help them.

"Well, it goes like 'Four, three, two, one,'' she said humming the tune.

I thought for a moment and knew exactly what song they were talking about.

"That sounds like Major Tom from Peter Schilling," I said. "I am not sure how you spell the last name but that definitely sounds like the song. And I don't know what album it is on. Your best bet would be going through some 80's compilation cds. Maybe it will turn up on one of them. But that is definitely the song."

They gave me the same strange look.

"Thanks… I guess," the one with the obsession said.

And that built my reputation as that guy with the useless knowledge of music. Word got around and people, mostly girls, would come to me and hum stuff, looking for some other way of identifying the noise polluting their minds.

Yes, I knew music. And movies. That's all I was obsessed with. This coming from some guy who didn't even have a VCR in his house until he was eight years old. And if my father ever caught me looking at the movies page in the newspaper, there would be hell to pay. No, he didn't want that sort of trash entering the mind of his son who was going to be a doctor.

Ah, how naive of my old man.

Chapter 55

I would go to the train station religiously. Taya Ji wanted me to go there like he had been doing all his life. If I was going to take over something he had been so passionate about then he made sure, I did it like he used to do it. Only difference was that I left the house a little later than he had done. He woke up everyday with the fajr azaan- that was the morning call to prayers.

It also woke me up but I always tried to go back to sleep. It took a while but I started getting used to waking up and then managing to fall back asleep. I wouldn't fully wake up until eight or so. Fajr went with the sunrise. So I would get a little more rest after the speakers at the local mosque quieted down.

Then I would get up, get cleaned up, have my morning glass of milk, and head off to the station. I didn't drink tea like Taya Ji did. I never drank tea.

Or coffee. I used to drink chocolate milk when I was living with my parents and kept up the ritual in the US. At Taya Ji's, it had taken some getting used to the taste of plain milk. Thank God, I had managed to get some Ovaltine from a store. The date on it had been scraped off, meaning it was probably expired.

But I just needed something to flavor the milk and that had been sufficient. But like I was saying, there was a difference in the taste of milk.

Taya Ji kept the milk in a covered bowl by the window sill since it was a little chilly those days. I had no idea how he was going to manage when it got warmer.

A milk man used to come on his bicycle every few days. A lot of times the milk would be watered down. Taya Ji would complain but the guy just said that it is how he had gotten it. I never tried to tell Taya Ji that in the US, people actually had this watered down milk for people on diets. But he wouldn't care about the "crazy Americans" and their "skim" milk.

Once at the train station, I would usually just sit around and wait. Good thing I had smoking to keep me occupied. My pack a day habit probably tripled over there... but I was a patient one. Smoke, wait, read, and wait some more. The usual people would end up coming. The usual, old fashioned types who didn't have phones. Yes, there were still plenty of those.

I never did mention how Marya Durani had managed to give me a nice chunk of money, unwittingly. Oh yeah, I had started playing her birthday in the lottery back in the US. February eleventh.

And one day 0211 had come out in the Pick 4. Didn't pay too much since it was all low numbers. But I had played it ten times boxed, meaning it could come out in any combination. 1102 had come out and paid around two hundred dollars. So I got around two thousand dollars cash. Converted into rupees, it had ended up being over a hundred thousand rupees. Sure it sounds like a lot but the way prices were in Pakistan, it wasn't going to last me too long. But I wasn't worried about that for now.

So it wouldn't be right of me to say that she gave me nothing. But I didn't want what I got. Sure it was coming in handy now but I would give it back ten fold if it meant giving it up would gain her. Then when I would think about it, I would realize that if things had somehow worked out with her, I wouldn't have come back to Taya Ji. The old man would have had to keep going on with his lonely existence. Did things work out for the better? I had no idea. I was actually quite angry about everything. Taya Ji had lived his life according to what he wanted to do. So what if it seemed desolate and lonely to others. He had been happy with it and that is all that counted. I thought so. And here I was trying to just do what I believed was right. And, to put it in a coarse manner, I was getting fucked over.

But maybe it was all my own doing. What if I had just gone along with what my parents had wanted. But that still left out the whole part about what I wanted. So I had no idea what I wanted. If only I could have just been set free to decide what it was, maybe I would have found something that was my calling. Then, maybe then, everyone could have been happy.

All this thinking drove me nuts. Which is why I would just sit there and smoke one cigarette after another. Sometimes, I would light one up from the one that was nearing its end. It just made me think of the time in the US when my friends had come to the conclusion that I was suffering from "depression." And I didn't like the idea that what was becoming of me was being dictated by a bunch of chemicals going haywire in my brain. No, I was depressed because that is how life was making me feel.

My school folder had a bunch of stuff scrawled all over it. Quotes, lyrics, and whatever made sense to me at the moment. One of the things that had appealed to me were the lyrics to a Tears for Fears song. There was a line in Mad World that just seemed so right. "I find it kind of funny/I find it kind of sad/the dreams in which I am dying/are the best I've ever had." Great song.

It made sense that people who had known me had started to feel that I needed help. But I knew me and I didn't feel that way. Like I had told one friend," I don't need help. I need a damn miracle."

Could it just be possible that maybe, just maybe, I did have some sort of chemical imbalance in my brain?

"I got this from my daughter in Dubai," Sajid sahib interrupted my train of misery.

"Sure," I said throwing away my cigarette and reaching for the letter. Yes, it was from his daughter in Dubai. She had been married to some guy who had gone and settled there a couple of years before their marriage. And in their three years of marriage she had popped out three kids. Two boys and a girl. At this rate, she would have a truck load by the time they had their tenth anniversary. But who was I to judge them. God bless them, I thought as I started reading the letter. It wasn't anything special.

The same old bullshit. They were doing well, the kids were all growing up fast, the oldest one had started school, they missed everyone back home, and they couldn't wait to see them again. Such banal stuff.

It was just so tempting to throw in something from my twisted mind. But I didn't do it. Just told the old man what it said. He got up smiling, gave me a fifty rupee bill, asked if it was sufficient, and made his way back home.

A part of me didn't want him to leave because I knew that he would be leaving me with someone I couldn't stand being with sometimes.

Myself.

Chapter 56

Why was it that everything that came my way turned out to be something that made me want to do something that was against everything I believed in? First, I wanted Marya Durani's marriage not to go through as intended. Then, once I realized she was definitely going to get married, I wanted her marriage to fall apart. As if she would get away from her wrecked marriage and come to me.

And now I was pining for another Marya who was already married. I, honest to God, hated what life threw my way and forced me to be.

But maybe there was a way around it. A way that I was choosing to ignore because of what seemed to be easier. But it wasn't easy, was it?

If I told my mother about my restlessness and unease at handling things in life, she would say that she knew exactly why I was so bothered. Its because I had turned my back on my religion. Islam was the way to live life. According to her, the only way to be at peace with myself and the world around me was to follow Allah's guidelines on living life. Live life according to what was in the Koran. It was true that if I started following blindly, it would be a lot easier. But I wasn't built like that. My mom always said that she prayed for God to guide me in the proper direction. I told her that maybe the Lord had already guided me in the right direction. Maybe He wanted me to be the way I was. As for me becoming a dedicated Muslim, I had a very simple solution for the whole problem. My mother was always praying. I told her that if she was such a big believer, all she had to do was pray that Allah shows me the way back to Islam. That's it.

She kept believing that one day, I would see the right way. That only meant that she believed I was headed the wrong way. I didn't want that. If anybody, it was my mother who should know that I wasn't doing anything wrong. But all she saw was me not being a Muslim. I wished that she could see it my way.

At least, she didn't think that I was a bad person. That turning away from Islam had made me some super-kafir, or non believer.

But I knew that I had good reason to step out of the Islamic circle. I had been on the inside. I had the knowledge. Only then did I decide to leave.

Maybe she had a point. If I had just gone along with the whole thing, I would be happy. But to me that would have been happiness in denial. Was that how I saw my fellow man? Blind creatures being led around by something they never totally grasped. Just decided to follow.

If that was so then that was another reason to hate myself. For seeing myself in a superior light. For thinking that I was above the rest for not having fallen into this trap. A trap set up by whom? I had no idea. I was so damn lost.

But I had gotten back in touch with my mom when I came back to Pakistan. I took a taxi to my parents' house in sector G-9/4 in Islamabad. That is how the city was set up. Into sectors. You could actually tell a lot about a person's social standing by what sector they lived in. The F and E sectors were where a lot of the rich people lived. My parents lived in the G sector and that is where I had grown up. It was mostly middle class and everyone there was our type. Hard working, middle class people living in their quiet neighborhoods. I had loved it there. But the school I had gone to was in the F sector. F-8/4 to be exact. The students there had been mostly from my kind of family. Middle class. But since it was the F sector, there were also some rich kids who seemed to always look down at my types who didn't live in the same sector as them. Eventually, we all got mixed in to a point where it didn't matter where one was from. There were kids coming on foot and there were kids being dropped off by their parents in luxury cars. Once inside, it didn't matter. But it probably sounds like some military set up with all these sectors. No, it was just how they had set the capital up.

But getting back to what I was saying, I went to pay my mother a visit. I took a taxi from where Taya Ji lived and went at a time when I knew my father wouldn't be home. I honestly didn't want to face my father. There was no possible way he would understand. I knew that my mother wouldn't understand either but mom's are always easier to deal with.

I got out of the taxi, gave the driver the money, and stood there looking at the house where I had grown up. Still looked the same. Two floors, grey color, and the same shade of marble covering the front side. Even the neighbors' houses looked the same. I walked up the slope of the driveway, and rang the bell. There was a gated entrance and the gate was locked since my mother would be home alone at the time. I just hoped that none of the neighbors would notice my arrival. I just wasn't ready to confront anyone. I heard the door open and saw my mother approaching the gate with a bit of hesitation since she wasn't expecting anybody.

As she neared the gate, she saw me through the rails, and obviously couldn't believe who she saw standing there.

"Irfan?" she finally uttered, her voice quivering a little.

"Yes, ami," I replied giving her a smile as she opened the small door that was in the gate to let people in and out.

"What are you doing here? What happened? Are you okay?" she started as she hugged me, ran her hand over my head, and kissed me on both cheeks.

It wasn't going to be easy, I thought as I stepped in through the door and closed it behind me.

"Well, I came back," I finally managed to say.

"But you just called me from America two days ago," she said. Now we were inside the house and I was looking around to see what kind of changes had taken place while I was gone. No change. The walls were still the same beige I had left. The furniture was still sparse and the TV was still that same nineteen inch Sanyo that I used to watch my cartoons on.

"I actually called you from a store by Taya Ji," I said. "I have been back for a while." Actually I had no idea how long I had been back.

"What about your college?" she said.

Yes, this was definitely not going to be easy.

"I left that, actually. I am staying with Taya Ji," I said.

"Why? What happened? Are you okay?" she just kept throwing questions at me.

"Nothing happened, ami," I said, trying to figure out how I was going to explain myself. "I just had enough of it and thought it would be a good change for me to come back and help out taya ji."

"But how are you living with him? He doesn't even have a bed in that shack of his," she said.

"Oh, its okay," I said. "I just sleep on the floor. Besides, he is getting old and I want to help him since you people never even check up on him."

"How can we be in touch with him?" she said. "He doesn't have a phone or anything. Besides he never contacts your father."

"But you can still give him a visit every now and then," I said.

"I don't know. Besides, he is your father's brother and he never even brings him up," she said.

"Well, he is pretty old and I thought that he could use my help. Please don't tell abu about this. I just wanted to come and see you," I said.

"Okay, beta," she said. "But when are you going to go back to your college?"

How could I tell her that I had no intention of going back? I was here and had no idea about where I was heading or what I was planning on doing.

"I don't know, ami," I said. "I just needed a break. And I have to go back to taya's since I didn't tell him I was coming here."

She gave me a fond look and I could see her eyes were welling up with tears. God, I should have known that this would end up happening. I gave her a hug and started walking out when she pulled me back by my shirt.

"What is this?" she said pulling me by my ear.

She had noticed the earring I had in my left ear.

"Oh, just did that to show I had been in America," I said pulling away from her and realizing again that maybe it hadn't been such a good idea to pay her a visit.

She started shaking her head and wiping away tears from her eyes. I had made my mother cry. I was a miserable person.

"Khuda Hafiz," I said walking towards the road. I would have to go back out to the main road to get another taxi.

"Allah Hafiz," my ami said.

I walked towards the main road thinking that this hadn't been such a good idea. I was a lousy son.

It took a few minutes but I finally saw a taxi. I signaled for the guy to stop and got in when he pulled up. I told him where to go and sat back He had some Urdu music playing and my guess would be that it was probably from some Indian movie that was popular those days. Like I mentioned before, I wasn't and had never been a fan of Urdu music or movies.

Thank God this driver wasn't one of those types that feels the need to carry on a conversation. He drove quietly and I just leaned my head back, closed my eyes, and thought about what was going on.

I had always been closer to my mother. Never really had too much to talk about with my father. Of course there were always those awkward moments when I found myself in a spot where I had to carry on a conversation with him. I hated those times because I never knew what to say to him. He had always been the serious type. Never really joked around about anything. All you could talk to him about was what you were planning to do with your life. Kids don't want to talk about that stuff. He was never into movies or music. And I had ended up becoming a huge follower of those two things. Was it just to spite my father? I hoped not. In fact, he was pretty much against the cinema and the worthless garbage that was entertaining the hordes.

Which is why we never had a VCR. I used to hear kids in school talk about what movies they had seen and found myself unable to relate to anyone focused on that aspect of life. For me, there were no movies.

On occasion, I would find myself able to catch the latest episodes of some American show that had been imported to the Pakistani airwaves. Knight Rider and Air Wolf were two of my favorites. Or I would be at a friend's house and be able to watch some movie they had rented. Action movies were what everyone was watching. Rambo was big and anything with Arnold Schwarzenegger was bigger. First Blood, Rocky, Over the Top, Terminator, and Commando. That was quality film fare. English language movies were popular but the Indian movies were a lot bigger.

For me, anything that seemed out of the ordinary junk that was on TV was good enough.

I sat in the taxi and thought about all that was going on. I was a lousy son. I felt terrible for my mother. All the dreams the poor lady had associated with me and I had given her nothing. No pretty daughter in law and no grandkids.

Poor lady. She deserved something better. But it wasn't all my fault, I thought trying to justify things. What about what I wanted? Its not like I was so happy with the way things were.

Shouldn't I be allowed to try to make something out of this life that I felt had been forced upon me. I didn't have a choice about being here. It just wasn't fair for me to be brought into this world and have all these expectations that I would have to fulfill for those who had brought me to the world.

No, it just wasn't fair. But then, it wasn't fair for my mother either. All she had done was what was expected of her and all she asked was for me to do what she was expecting of me. But it wasn't fair.

That is all I had to say to myself about being myself.

Chapter 57

"Read this," an abrupt female voice jolted me out of my daze.

It was some old lady standing there holding out a letter. Actually, I was guessing she was old from her voice since I couldn't really see her face. She had a black burqa on. Those were the dresses worn by the really religous types which covered them from head to toe. All they would have was the opening in front of their eyes so they could see.

I could tell from the wrinkly hands that she must be quite old. And from the looks of those wrinkly hands, I didn't she needed that burqa. She wouldn't be the type to set male hormones haywire.

There I went again. Judging someone just from that instant. I had no right to have thought what I had just thought.

"Sure," I said taking the letter from her outstretched hand. "Have a seat."

I read the thing to her word for word like she told me to. Same old stuff that I had gotten used to reading from these people. A son, this time in Riyadh, Saudi Arabia, writing about how he was working so hard and saving up the money to come back home. How his missed his family.

Mom, dad, and brother. No wife was mentioned so I guessed he was still unmarried. I did my job, accepted the fifty rupees she gave, thanked her, and went back into my mind. That place I had started to hate being in.

I thought of my mother. I thought of a way I could possibly make her happy while holding on to what could make me happy as well. That's where the problem was. I didn't have anything to hold on to that could make me happy. I was an utter failure, I thought. I had abandoned my parents' hopes trying to reach something that would eventually make us all happy. Instead, I had just gotten more miserable. Now it wasn't just about me being unable to make them happy. Now I didn't see any possibility of making them or myself happy.

I looked at my hands and the small scars on my wrist. That's all they were. Small scars. I had wanted to just die after Marya. I constantly thought about ending a life that didn't seem to be nearing a natural end anytime soon. I would use small razors to make myself bleed. I had heard that if you were going to slit your wrists, it was better to slash them vertically. Then it would be harder to stitch them back and undo what had been intended. But the scars on my wrist were all horizontal. And small. A further sign of the failure that I was. Couldn't even go through with that bit. It was my parents' fault. That is how I tried to rationalize it. I didn't want their only son to leave them like that. Sure, that was it. I was a good son.

But was Marya worth dying for? I tried not to think so. More justifications for what I couldn't do.

Slitting my wrists was the only option I had come to for ending my life. I could have hanged myself. But there was that problem of where to do it. It had to be done in my apartment but the problem there was a bare ceiling. There was nothing there to tie the rope to. Plus I didn't have any rope handy. See, I wasn't even dedicated to this. I had to have rope handy to do it. I could have gotten some of that twine that they used at the Patels' store to tie up old papers. But there was no way it could have held my weight. And there were two problems with sleeping pills, which seemed to be the most peaceful option. One, I would need a prescription, since pills weren't distributed so easily in the US. In Pakistan, it would have been so much easier. The second problem with sleeping pills was a little idiotic paranoia. What if they didn't really kill you? So you took a bunch of them and people figured you were dead. But what if you were just really fast asleep. Everything would be done, the funeral, the crying, and you actually woke up. But it was too late since you were already buried. That would really suck, my idiotic mind rationalized. Shoot myself? Getting a gun could be just as difficult as those pills without a prescription.

And I had no idea about how to use a gun. With my luck, I would probably end up shooting myself in the foot.

Yes, there weren't too many options. Slitting my wrists seemed to be the only feasible choice. And all that ended up doing was making me wear long sleeved shirts regardless of how warm it was so nobody could get a glimpse of those scars on my wrist.

Yes, I totally sucked at life and any ability to end it.

So I gave up on giving up. Maybe if I tried harder, things would go my way. That was around the time I decided to leave the US and go back to Pakistan to live with my favorite Taya Ji.

If the suicidal urges were gone then why was I still smoking. That had been my original intent when I started smoking. A slow demise. But friends urged me to stop smoking because it wasn't like you just smoked and died. Things could be a lot worse before the end hit. The perfect example for me would be the old man Benny. He used to hang out at Josh's Pub. Must have been in his seventies and had given up smoking the hard way when he had developed emphysema. But he still loved his beer. So he was there almost every night with his oxygen tank beside him. Josh actually got mad at him because there he'd be with his oxygen tank, surrounded by a bunch of people who usually had a cigarette in their hand. Josh had actually kicked him out of the place a couple of times but the old man was resilient. He would be gone a couple of nights and then be back on the third. Eventually, Josh gave up on trying to reason with this walking fire hazard. They compromised and Benny would just at the end of the bar, away from everyone else. All us regulars felt bad for the old man and always went and sat by him without our cigarettes. He loved his beer and he loved to talk. He would just go on and on about his younger days and all the women he had loved. Looking at him then, it was hard to believe that this grandpa type had done all he said. He told us stories from his younger days and how he had managed to nail so many "floozies."

But there he was now, single, old, and so much closer to the end, then the rest of us young ones. Actually he put things in perspective for us. About how life was such a transitional phase.

We laughed at his stories, took some advice, got our buzz, left the place, and forgot all about what he had said by the time we woke up the next morning.

Chapter 58

Somehow, somewhere, I decided to give life another shot. I wasn't going to die over that bitch Marya Durani.

That's when I realized what she had done. She made me call her a bitch. At least, in my head, I had thought of her as being a bitch. For leading me on. For not letting me know the truth - that she was already taken. The bitch had led me on.

And on top of it all, she made me hate myself for thinking of her in that term. I didn't want to think of her like that but I didn't see a choice in the matter. But had she really led me on? Or was I to blame for seeing something that wasn't even there. Maybe she was just being civil to someone she had met in a foreign land.

That was it. She was just being nice to me. It was I who had misinterpreted it as being something that it wasn't.

Fine. She didn't have to be my girlfriend and future wife. She could just be my girl friend. Two separate words.

It was really that easy. There weren't any ulterior motives behind my fondness. She didn't have to put out. She could just be what most of the females that I had known had been. Friends. Maybe I just wasn't the boyfriend type. Girls had told me that throughout my life. Not bluntly. Just said that I was a real good friend as they had walked off behind the bleachers while holding the hand of some guy I knew was about to get some.

And I had always just smiled, brushed it off as the way it was meant to be, and moved on.

But this Marya had made me reach my boiling point. I didn't want to be that nice guy that girls could just trust and confide in. I wanted to be someone that they would confide with their friends about.

But I wasn't going to die over her. I was going to give life another chance. As if it needed one from me. Like I was the one calling the shots.

No, I realized. I was adrift in this thing called life.

❦

"What happened to you?" Harry asked me as I walked into the store to start my shift at 9 am.

Harry was actually Harish Patel, the owner of that little store I had started working at. The one I have been addressing as Mr. Patel. He must have been in his late fifties. I had never asked him. It didn't matter to me.

"Oh, I fell," I said. This was the day after my attempt at ending my life. Actually, I can't even call it an attempt. Attempts have some effort behind it. This had just been a trial version of suicide. I had finally settled on slitting my wrists as the available and convenient option. And all I had managed to do was put some small slits on my left wrist. Just drew a little blood. It had ended up being more of an inconvenience since I had to wash that hand clean, clean off the small cuts with some rubbing alcohol, and put some Band-Aids on them. Not just any Band-Aids. Looney Tune band aids that I had picked up at the local pharmacy and kept in my bathroom in case I ever needed them.

"How did you manage to fall and hurt your wrist?" Harry inquired further.

"Oh, I went out the back door at Josh's and its a little rough in the parking lot back there," I said hoping to end this conversation as soon as I could.

"So you must have had a couple too many brewskis," he said laughing.

"Nah," I said thinking about why I didn't just agree with the old man and end the thing. "I just missed a step since I am not really used to going out that back way."

"You have to be careful, boy," Harry said as a customer walked in and I thanked God for providing this distraction.

The guy just bought a pack of gum, left a quarter on the counter, and walked out while glancing at the magazines on the wall. He didn't see any dirty ones so he didn't stand there and browse. Yes, the Patels didn't have any porn in their store. They used to, but the local church had come to them a couple of years ago and requested that they stop selling such material.

They had agreed and the church had give them a framed sign that said, "PORN FREE!!! FAMILY CONVENIENCE STORE." They had the sign proudly displayed on the wall near the magazines.

Some guys that I had gotten to be friendly with were always complaining to me about the lack of such material. I told them that I wasn't the owner and, frankly, was glad that I didn't have to put up with the type of people who would come for that stuff. Although there was this old guy who would come in every couple of weeks and ask if we had "Busty" magazine.

No sir, I always told that dirty old man.

Thank God, that guy who came in for the gum, distracted Mr. Patel from the condition of my wrists.

"Okay, I will be going then," he said. "There are no deliveries today. The milk guy came already. Just keep an eye on the kids after school."

He started walking out the door as I took my seat by the cash register. He was almost out the door when he stopped, turned around, and said," thank you, Irfan."

"Oh, you are welcome, sir," I replied as I always had when he showed gratitude which I didn't see as necessary.

He finally left and I sat back in the chair, hoping nobody would come in for at least ten or fifteen minutes. Thank God, I got my wish.

And this was my other home. The little convenience store that used to be operated by Harry and his wife Meena. Nice people, I had always thought even before I started working there. Harry was in his fifties.

Maybe late fifties, I think, since I had never asked him his age. It wasn't important. His wife must have been in her forties. Once again, I am guessing since I never asked them their ages. All I know is that they had a son who was twenty eight years old and a daughter who was also around the mid-twenties. The daughter had been married to some guy in India and she was still there, busy having kids. I think she had two girls and two boys already.

The son was the reason that the Patels had come to the US. So they could get him a good education and set him on a nice career path. He had done well and ended up becoming a doctor. I think he was a hematologist or something like that. Yes, I didn't pay too much attention to other people's affairs. I just minded my own business. All I knew was that the son was now working for some hospital in New York City and wasn't too keen on going back to India to get married like his parents had hoped and planned. At least, he still visited them every weekend. The parents had bought this store with they money they had brought over from India fifteen or so years ago. Now they were, pretty much, stuck operating the place on their own. Their labors had worked out and their son was a success. The only thing was that now he was on his own while the parents were still there running the store. He was a doctor now and didn't want any part of what had put him through college and medical school.

Good thing my lost self had come along and started working for the Patels. Yes, I did pat myself on the back for helping out these people. But having this little job was a great help to me as well. And they paid me five dollars an hour cash, under the table. I didn't file any taxes and the money helped me pay my rent, put some food in my belly, and gas in the car. That is all I was looking for. I didn't have any special needs except for my alcohol fix at night.

I was a simple man.

I remembered when I used to be a simple boy. Things had definitely changed.

I guess I was a simple man now. I hated being called the "m" word. It pushed so much responsibility on a person. In my head, I was still a boy. I still loved my cartoons. No, I wasn't too big on the cartoons that were on TV at the time. The Ninja Turtles or whatever

Crap - to me they were just infomercials for toys. My cartoons were the old school stuff. Looney Tunes, Rocky and Bullwinkle, and whatever used to entertain me as a kid. It still held my interest.

But the kids in the US were so spoiled with all the choices they had. In Pakistan, when I was growing up, TV didn't start until three in the afternoon. And it ended at ten at night. Plus there was only one channel. And it was usually full of dry stuff that didn't interest me at all.

But I would sit there in front of the TV and watch it religiously, because you never knew when a cartoon would pop up. If I went away for a little while, I would miss it. Because they were just mini cartoons. Like an episode of Tom and Jerry. Or maybe Heckle and Jeckle, the two talking and mischievous magpies. I loved my cartoons. I was never going to grow out of that. I didn't want to.

Once I had moved out of my aunt and uncle's place after I turned eighteen, I had gotten my own little apartment in Ridgewood. They had a lot of apartment complexes there and most of them were occupied by immigrants who were using them as stepping stones on their way to achieving their American dream. The supers didn't care about doing their jobs as long as they got paid. That is why there were some one bedroom apartments with seven or eight people living in them.

I could never put up with that. So I had gotten myself a small one bedroom apartment as soon as I turned eighteen. I had to wait a year after graduating from high school since, unlike everyone else, I was only seventeen when I graduated. Maybe my mother had wanted to get me out of the house quick and put me in school at a younger age than other kids. Who knew? I told my aunt and uncle that I needed a little buffer zone between high school and college; some time to figure out where I was headed. Thank God, they went along with it. They even convinced my parents back in Pakistan to let me do as I wanted. It wouldn't be good to pressure me into something I wasn't ready for. I should be allowed to do it my way. Thank God, they thought I was sensible enough. Were they wrong? I hate to say it, but maybe they should have forced me to do something I didn't want. Maybe it would have been better for me in the long run. Maybe I was better off being led into something that would eventually benefit me instead of being allowed to choose. Because I made bad choices.

I was such a fuck up.

Chapter 59

I was sitting behind the counter, leaning forward with my chin resting on the cold top when I noticed some movement outside.

Some customer was finally going to come in. I looked out the window and saw a black pick-up pulling up, with the words DUN WELL ELECTRIC on the side. Yes, it was Richie the electrician coming in for his morning usual.

I always made fun of his company name. How can it be "done well" when its not even spelled well? He used to laugh it off.

"What's up, Sandi?" he said walking in.

I just pointed to the ceiling and then said," you know that is really racist."

Sandi is what he called me a lot of times. It was short for "sand nigger" which was something I would sometimes call myself and shock the white majority around me.

"Just shut up," Richie said as he walked towards the coffee counter in the middle of the store. "You call yourself that all the time. Besides it was your idea shortening it to 'sandi'."

Well, at least this was going to wake me up and get my mind off of my life.

"You need to understand proper race etiquette," I said as he put five spoonfuls of sugar in his coffee. "I can call myself whatever I want. I can even call other people, that are my shade, that. Just like black people are always calling each other 'nigga.' But you, white boy, can't call us those names. I don't know who came up with those rules but that is the way it is. So suck it up, cracker."

"Oh, you can call me cracker?," he asked, putting his coffee on the counter.

I reached up and took down a pack of GPC Menthols for him. "Yes, I can, white boy. Because I am the minority and you people are the majority. And you know what, they say that menthols are favorites of the black population."

"Bull," he said reaching into his pocket for the total I had rung up.

I gave him his change and said, "You know I am just kidding right?"

"Oh, I know, sand man," he said laughing as he headed towards the door.

I needed that.

I needed that because it let me hold on to a little bit of myself. I had somehow built a reputation for never being serious. I could be dying inside but I had to keep it to myself. Yes, I was extremely stoic. It was one of those things that I prided myself at being. And it was one of those things that I hated myself for being. I, honest to God, didn't want to keep it in me. I wanted to let it out. But I had no way of letting it out. I had held it in for so long that I had forgotten how to let it out.

My mind was set that if I was ever going to let it out, it had to be to the one, i.e. the one I was going to spend the rest of my life with. Yes, I am back to my obsession with the heart being a lonely hunter. My existence of denial. Maybe I hadn't really fallen in love with Marya. Maybe I was just so pathetically alone that I had chosen her as being the one. Maybe it wasn't love. Maybe it was just the utter need for someone.

Yes, I was pretty screwed. Sitting here in this strange land.

No wonder I had become so obsessed with Stranger in a Strange Land. At least up to the point where it had ended up being too much science fiction. I had loved the humanity that was brought upon its alien protagonist. Something I had definitely been able to relate to. Being in this strange land that people in Pakistan were dying to get to. If they only knew. Being impoverished was a small price to pay for having the sanity that they all had. But they didn't appreciate that. They all wanted to come to America. Everything was so much better in America. Right? Sure, if you were willing to stop being who you were. If you were willing to become something you were not.

The US was great. It was great if you could just be what you were supposed to be. It would have all been great if I had just gone on being what I was supposed to be.

For all immigrants, there are two choices.

Either stay true to your origins or become Americanized. But was becoming Americanized a form of selling out? No, because that country was giving you a second chance at life. Becoming a loyal American wasn't a form of selling out. It was the right thing to do. But what about turning your back on who you were? Was it right to just forget about your origin and get swept up in the newfound pleasures?

Was my parents' fear of their son marrying some American, a form of prejudice? Did they do so because of an inherent belief that their culture was superior to the others?

Everybody was prejudiced. But not me. I was somehow cursed with this notion that I had to look at everyone as being above me. I was lowly and had to bring myself up to the level of those around me.

Low self esteem? Well, if you want to call it that.

Chapter 60

"Really?," Mr. Martin said looking at me with eyes that seemed to be questioning my mental well-being.

"No, it was just normal," I replied as the rest of the class gave me the same look that he was giving me.

It was Mr. Martin's world history class and all of us tenth graders were sitting there trying not to doze off with his dry delivery of the day's topic, the role played by the military in the governments past and present.

It had just occurred to him that I was from Pakistan and that he should ask me about a country that had been under martial law for a nice amount of time.

"So your family was okay when Zia was in power?" he asked.

"Sure, they were okay. I was there and we seemed to do fine," I replied.

I think that everybody in the class started looking at me in a different way after that day. As some tough survivor who had lived through a terrible time in his native country's past.

"But you didn't have any of the freedom which you now enjoy?," the old timer persisted in what appeared to be his attempt to make me say how brutal it had been. Maybe even bring me to tears recalling the torturous past.

"I did whatever I wanted and so did my parents," I said hoping to move to some different topic.

And I was not brushing him off with some vague answers. That was the God's honest truth. Once again, I thought of the people surrounding me as being plain spoiled. Here they were, living in the

United States, and without a clue about what the world out there was like.

Yes, I had lived under martial law. No, it had not been terribly suffocating. Maybe its because my family wasn't resistant. Maybe they just lived simply and went along with the way things were. Maybe I was from a bunch of cowards who didn't fight for their rights. But, honestly, I had not known that martial law was so terrible until I had come to the US and was told that it was by others.

Zia ul Haq, no relation to me even though we had the same last name, was an army general who had taken over the country after throwing Zulfiqar Bhutto out of power and executing him. His army had become the rule. And things had been fine. After his death, (an accidental plane crash or the job of a saboteur), things had gotten a lot worse as Bhutto's daughter Benazir had come back from England and decided to enter the political arena. The election fiasco had happened and she had become the Prime Minister, though the electoral outcomes could never be trusted in a corrupt system like the one Pakistan had.

But in the US, she had so many admirers. People spoke of her like she had been an angel. I thought that she had been a terrible leader. I was young but could still notice how terrible things had gotten since she came to power. I think Americans just liked her because she had managed to do so much as a female.

That's it. She did a lot but was any of it good? I, as someone who had been in it, didn't think so.

But try explaining that to the people in a country which had failed to produce a female leader despite all its advances and female empowerment.

No, not easy. So I never tried.

Chapter 61

I can't really pinpoint when it was that I started drifting away from my religious upbringing. No, I wasn't being raised to become a religious leader, or maulwi, as they were called. I just was never comfortable with any of it. I was eight years old when I finished reading the Koran - all thirty siparas, or chapters. Yes, it was a big deal. My parents had a big gathering with all their friends there to celebrate. They all congratulated me, praised me, and gave me gifts. I must have gotten close to a thousand rupees which was a pretty big deal to me. I laughed, I smiled, and I acted all happy.

Yes, I acted happy. Maybe I was a little happy since it was good to see my family being proud of something I had done. But why was the happiness so flimsy? Because I had read the entire Koran but could hardly tell anyone what was in it. I had read it in Arabic and I didn't speak or understand the language. Yes, I could read it like you reading this might be able to read Spanish, Italian, Polish, or so many other languages. But being able to read something doesn't mean that there is understanding.

So my issue became that I should be able to read the Koran in Urdu. At least that way, I would know what it was that I was reading.

No, I was supposed to learn Arabic and read it so there wouldn't be anything lost in translation. Fine.

But then I got a spanking in school when I was in second grade.

"What were you talking about?" Madam Kausar said when she saw me sitting in her class talking to Saleem behind me.

"Oh, Saleem was being a jerk," I started to reply but was cut short by a slap on the face. It was not the first time I had gotten slapped but maybe it was the unexpectedness that made it burn more than the other times. Other times I had deserved it for being mischievous but this time I had no idea what had brought it upon me.

"How many times do I have to tell you that its Abdul Saleem," Madam Kausar said in a loud voice.

"I am sorry," I said in a voice teetering on hurt.

Yes, it had been my fault. I wasn't supposed to address Saleem as Saleem. Especially not when calling him a jerk.

In the Koran, Allah was addressed by around one hundred different names. All of them praising his greatness, of course.

Saleem was one of them. To address somebody who had been given one of those names by just that name was blasphemous to those who were strict Muslims. The proper way of addressing someone with that name was to add "Abdul" to the front. Like Abdul Sami, or Abdul Wahid. Abdul meant "man of," in Arabic. So you weren't calling somebody the Almighty. You were calling them the Almighty's man.

Yes, that was it. That was why I had gotten slapped.

But Saleem was a jerk. And now he was an even bigger jerk because of what had happened because of him.

So it was these little things that kept pushing me away from Islam. God forbid, I didn't set out to be like that. It was just how it happened. Like it was meant to be. Like the Lord was dropping hints for me to follow.

Maybe I was meant to be lost.

But I realized later that I was so lucky for being slapped around by a female teacher. Yes, it did hurt when you were seven years old but it got worse when the male teachers took over. The female hand, no matter how hard it hit you, still had a gentler quality. Later on, when the male teachers took over, the difference became more obvious. Their slaps were not only harder but also had a stronger wind behind them. Make sense? It's probably not going to make sense to anyone who dialed up the cops when mom raised her voice at them.

But I remembered those days. I still felt the burning on my cheeks sometimes. I would touch my face whenever I thought about those days. And for some strange reason, I would always smile when I thought about those days. Maybe because now it seemed funny. Or maybe the smile meant a fond recollection of those good old days.

Good old days?

Yes, I missed those days.

"Hello," a female voice brought me out of my stupor.

I was sitting at the train station, waiting for some lost soul to bring me their woes in writing. Nobody came so I drifted into my mind.

"Hello," I said as I opened my eyes and found that I had my left hand on my cheek.

Yes, it was embarrassing. Especially since the voice that had brought me to attention belonged to Marya.

Chapter 62

Let me pat myself on the back and say that I had to have been the Patel's dream employee. I didn't ask for anything. Honestly. They just had to pay me five dollars an hour, under the table. That's it. And I didn't even demand it. They could give it to me whenever. If business was slow, which it was, they could pay me after they had paid off their more important bills.

After all, my parents were sending me money for my school. Yes, I wasn't going to school but the money was coming every month.

Did I feel guilty about keeping them in the dark about what was actually going on?

Sometimes. But then I justified it for myself by saying that it was their idea to send me to the US. My opinion didn't count when the decision was made. I was the stupid child who didn't know about the great choices being made for him by mom and dad. Forget guilt. I actually felt that they owed me this much, at least. For tearing me away from my friends and shipping me off to this land of temptations that I wasn't supposed to succumb to… Why? Because they had apparently done a good job in raising me as someone who wouldn't be sucked into all the sins that were so abundant in America. No, I was just going to be a good boy, get my education, and return to Pakistan where a good job and beautiful wife would be waiting for me. It was almost like Allah's game plan on a much smaller scale.

If I was a good Muslim, there would be all these good things and beautiful virgins in the afterlife. Yes, that was it. Their religion had somehow seeped into their earthly life. They were playing God by asking me to be what they wanted.

If I seem a little resentful, maybe its because I was.

But maybe my parents' upbringing had failed in the theology department. Maybe they couldn't raise me to be the Muslim that they were expecting.

But maybe some of the other things they had wanted to instill in me had somehow rubbed off on me. I think my honesty came from them. I will give them that much…

So ami and abu deserved that much credit. And I hated them for making me hate myself for doing anything that I knew was going against their wishes. If it was so right for me to be my own person, then why was their guilt attached to every action that seemed to be my own personal calling?

I had no idea. Did I try to grasp any hint of an idea? No, it was easier to just go with the way it was going and be constantly tortured by the oppressive feelings of guilt that came with it.

I think I tried to quit smoking a couple of times. I didn't go back because of a craving. I went back because it just seemed so right to give my body something, that was helping the brain controlling it, a reason to go on.

Yeah, that was it. I wasn't addicted.

At Josh's Pub, they always had my things ready whenever they saw me park my car. Either the front side or in the back parking lot, I was visible. Whenever I walked in, my shot of RumpleMinze would be sitting there in a rocks glass with the ashtray next to it. I had started getting the shot in a rocks glass because the shot glasses were too small and I had spilled it quite a few times.

Gina, one of the girls who worked on the weekend suggested it and I had stuck to it. No rocks, or ice cubes as they are better known, in my drink since it was already chilled and those rocks just took up space in the glass.

I just wasn't a beer drinker since I had never liked the taste. But that didn't stop Josh from nicknaming me "Beerfan." Whatever.

He had actually gotten mad at me in the beginning because I complicated things for his lazy ass. I used to go for mixed drinks. A Mudslide (personal favorite), a Jolly Rancher, or the most hated of all, a Long Island Iced Tea. That last one was especially hated since it had so many ingredients. Honestly, I couldn't tell you a single one of those ingredients. But a friend had pulled it as a suggestion for getting hammered, off of the Internet and I had liked it. Yes, it got the job done. But, according to Josh, his place was a "beer and shot" bar that didn't appreciate people going for those "faggoty-ass" drinks. But I managed to get served to my liking. In the course of my finishing the LIT, I must have gone through half a pack of cigarettes.

Yes, the self-destruct cycle was in full action after Marya. She had ended up becoming a steady email contact and I would tell her about how strong a buzz I got on any given night. I was dying and she could save me. A big mistake, according to the friends I confided in... They said that it just scared away any potentials. But in my genius psyche, she was going to recognize it as a call for help. She would see how in love with her I was and come rushing back to be with me.

Maybe it was true what they said about alcohol killing brain cells.

"So is it true that you Muslims are required to kill those who are not?", Gregg said in a slurred manner that meant he was nearing the point where Josh would cut him off.

"No," I said hoping not to get too deep into it.

"No, I know for a fact that it is part of your religion. To kill all the infidels. Anybody who doesn't switch over to Muslim," he continued, not satisfied by my response. "What do they call it, Jihad or some thing like that."

Maybe I had had a few too many as well, since I decided to go into an explanation. It wouldn't matter because I highly doubted he would remember much of what was said in response to what was asked.

"Yeah, Jihad is one of the five pillars of Islam but I think its gotten a bad rep," I started as I put out one cigarette and pulled another one out of the pack. "But it doesn't really mean that you go on a holy war against those who are not Muslims. It just means that you defend your religion with your life. In fact, it even tells you to not even chop down a tree that is in your path on your way to battle."

Why the hell was I defending something that even I didn't believe in any more? I had no idea. Just that it was a favorite habit of mine to try to prove people wrong. I should have joined the debate team in school but there were just to many rules. I liked the no rules type of arguments where it could even come down to fists flying as a form of rebuttal. Thank God, it had never come to that.

"Really," Gregg said as he put down his empty bottle of Molson Ice and signaled to Josh for another.

"Dude," Josh said shaking his head," I think you have had enough. I wouldn't mind but the cops are already on my case because some kids managed to get a six pack from one of the girls who work on the weekend."

Surprisingly, Gregg didn't protest. Just got off his stool, left a couple of dollars on the bar as tip, and walked towards the back door, quietly.

"You gonna be long, Irfan?" Josh said turning to me since I was the only one left in the bar on that dead Wednesday night.

"Whenever, just tell me," I said.

I hated leaving this place because I knew I would be spending the rest of the time with my thoughts, my guilt, and my memories. Sure there were some good memories but none had been coming to me lately.

I think it was easy to diagnose me as a manic depressive. Or just depressive since the manic part didn't seem to be around that much.

I was going to go home, turn my computer on, check my email and hope that there would be an email from Marya, telling me that she had abandoned her marriage and was coming back to the US to give me another chance. Yeah, she had to have been married by now. Unless, she had changed her mind. Yeah, wishful thinking.

I checked my email, found the inbox empty, and just went to bed. I went to bed to sleep but ended up lying there for a couple of hours with no signs of sleep lingering anywhere. I was tired but the mind was racing. Me and my head full of ghosts.

Chapter 63

For some reason, I always thought of myself as being worthy of punishment. Was it a self esteem thing? Was I just a masochist?

I have no idea.

But back to the five pillars of Islam - the five things that make you a good Muslim. One is having faith in Allah as the almighty and Mohammed as his prophet. Next comes the prayer or "namaaz" five times a day. Third is fasting during the month of Ramadan. Number four is giving alms to the needy. And last up is the Haj or pilgrimage to Mecca where hundreds of thousands of Muslims go every year. Mecca is in Saudi Arabia so it always struck me as a conspiracy by the Arabs to boost their economy. But I was talking about my masochistic side, wasn't I?

Of the five pillars of Islam, the one that I followed most eagerly was the fasting. I must have been around eight or so when I started fasting during the month of Ramadan. And Islamic fasting is tough. No food or water from sunrise to sunset. And since the Islamic calendar follows the moon, Ramadan can fall any time of the year.

There would be a year when Ramadan was in December. Easy, since the days are short and there isn't any heat to make you thirsty or fatigued. But then there would be years when Ramadan would fall right smack in the middle of summer. Now that was tough... It was hot as all hell and the days would be long. That's when I loved fasting. Because it drained me. My mouth would be dry and sweat would make me take a shower a couple of times a day. Thank God, you weren't forbidden from doing that.

I would be exhausted and feel like dying. I loved it. Sure I could spend the whole days sitting in an air conditioned room but this was Pakistan. During summer there would be a lot of

"load shedding." What is that? That's when the electric company shut off the power to make it easier for the availability of power where it was needed. Hospitals and schools? No, where

the rich people lived. And my family was not that rich. Thank God we were okay but hardly fitting the rich description. Middle class was more like it.

So we would sit there in the heat without any air conditioning or even ceiling fans. I would be miserable but deep down there would be a feeling that it was all good. A feeling that I deserved this misery.

Remember that this was way back before I had even heard of this thing called depression. All in all, everything was good and there wasn't any reason for me to feel depressed. But when I found out about this thing called depression, I was actually glad that there was a name that could be attached to what I had started classifying as normal feelings.

My mother used to get angry at me when all I did during Ramadan was fast.

"Its like you are just dieting," she used to say. "Allah doesn't want you to just starve yourself. You are supposed to read the Koran and, at least, say your prayers. You don't do anything. Just starve yourself."

Was it the guilt that made me go to the neighborhood mosque a couple of times every day? Or was I just trying to get her off my case? I think it was the later because I never did concentrate during my namaaz. Just participated in the ritual, which it was to me. Bow by head when the time came, get down on my knees, put my forehead to the ground, say the verses that went with the actions, and think about why I couldn't put my heart into it. There were others in the mosque but it was never too busy during the week. Friday was the big day when everybody descended on the mosques.

By everybody, I mean all the males. The females said their prayers at home. But I do remember hearing about the women going to their own mosque sometimes. Ones that were just for women. But I never saw my mother leave the house for prayers.

The other pillar of Islam that I liked was the one involving the giving of alms to the poor. Yes, I always felt that was the one useful thing in the religion. After the Friday prayers, there would usually be a few fakirs, or beggars, sitting outside the mosque. Some people would throw some money into their bowls while others would just walk by, ignoring them and feeling that they had already earned their spot in heaven by participating in the prayers.

Most probably, it was the only time they said their prayers in the entire week. Even then, they had probably come to the mosque hoping that they would meet some acquaintance they hadn't seen in a while.

But what all of us kids waited for every year during Ramadan was the end. That would be the big holiday when all the kids got money from the elders. No, there was no exchanging of gifts like at Christmas time. Only the kids got money from the grown ups. Cash money.

But things got a little frustrating because there was no fixed date for the end. The new moon had to be seen by the religious elders so they could announce the end of Ramadan. No, it didn't matter what the meteorologist said. The new moon had to be seen. Otherwise no eid. That was what the holiday marking the end of Ramadan is called. Eid al Fitr. And that is when, in my opinion, a shameful thing happened a lot. Some would celebrate eid because they had seen the moon while others would not celebrate because they hadn't. The biggest holiday of the Muslim year and they couldn't be united. A shame, I thought.

Although some people seemed to see that in a positive way. Why be so square like the Christians, celebrating their Christmas on the twenty-fifth of December every year?

Hey, at least they were united in their celebrations unlike the Muslims who I didn't see as getting anywhere. Not that I was starting to lean towards Christianity. But if I had my pick, I would probably end up becoming a Christian.

Once again, I was not judging the religion from the outside. I considered myself a defector. One who had been on the inside and chosen to step out.

Thank God, I wasn't some famous celebrity speaking his mind. Maybe then the Iranians or some other Muslim fanatics would put a price on my head.

I was just a nobody treating life as a multiple choice test. Stupid, yes, but oh so right for the moment.

Chapter 64

How the hell was I going to do this?

That was the only thing that had been in my head since I had met Marya at Josh's Pub. I had always been the single fellow, uninterested in any sort of female companionship while scared to death of going through life on his own. What the hell did they mean when they had said that there is a right time for things like that?

Things like finding another to share your life with. If this wasn't the right time then why was everything inside me telling me that this was it. I honestly had been willing to go along with what I had been brought up to be like... But that was until I had fallen so hard for that bitch. Did I just call her a bitch? I sure did. Because that is all I managed to see her as. That temptress, that siren, that bitch... Coming into my tranquil life to make it hell. But she didn't do anything. That was it. She didn't do anything. Just came, went, and left me in shreds.

Not only did my alcohol intake go up but my mind kept wanting to try something stronger and harder.

"Why don't you get some Everclear?" I asked Josh.

"Because you are going to try that shit, get drunk off your ass, and leave me with the leftover," Josh replied angrily.

Friends had told me that Everclear was the strongest thing out there. Rumple Minze was close but shots of that weren't doing anything for me anymore. Maybe my tolerance had gone up.

"Well, others will buy it, I am sure," I said.

"No, because it tastes like shit and I can't use it to make any mixed drinks," Josh said.

He did have a point. People who came to his place weren't looking for a quick drunken stupor. They wanted to enjoy it while losing it.

Except for me, of course. I didn't want to enjoy it because I didn't see myself as being able to enjoy anything.

I just wanted to lose it - It being all remnants of what might have been. Of what could have been.

But I was still cautious about how far I was willing to go. I didn't even try to get high or stoned or whatever the hip term for smoking a joint was nowadays.

Friends were branching out into things that I hadn't even heard of. The best, according to Jim, was Ecstasy. Apparently it had earned that name rightfully.

They were going to some clubs in New York City to get that stuff but if I was willing to try it, an interstate delivery could be arranged.

No thanks is all I kept saying even though the temptation was there. If anything, I was going to smoke a joint first. I never did, though.

Maybe the rumors of me being a pussy had some merit to them.

So getting my hands on any Everclear was out. I could get it if I tried, I was sure. But maybe it was just one of those things that I wanted to be there as an option that I didn't want to turn to. An option that seemed desirable. Hell, if I wanted to get hammered, I could just drink a lot of what was available to me. But I never did that. It was pretty strange. What the hell was I trying to do to myself? I didn't have a clue. I was proud to say that I had never gotten drunk to a point where I didn't know what was going on. So a part of me was fixated with staying in control while a part of me wanted to lose it. The former part won, thank God, since I don't think I ever wanted to be in a position where I wasn't in control any more.

I had no control of life and what it dealt me. So I tried to keep the control of whatever little that had been put in my hands. Something that I believed the good Lord wanted me to control.

Meaning I never did get my hands on any Everclear.

Just drank my couple of Molson Ices, got that light headed feeling that seemed so liberating at the time, and went out the door.

Two beer queer, as some would say. Fine. So be it. I never had and was never going to try to impress anyone. Maybe that's what my problem was.

Maybe I should have tried to impress Marya. Maybe if she had seen some effort on my part, she would have given it a second thought. What the hell am I doing talking about second thoughts? How about just a thought. An initial thought. Something that could be catapulted into something more. But I had to be so nonchalant. Act like I didn't really care. Keep it in me. Be the stoic that I had somehow ended up becoming.

If only she could have gotten a peek at the desperate boy inside me. The desperate boy longing to keep her. No. It had all happened for a reason. A reason that I had no inkling about. Maybe to make me miserable... If that was the reason then things were definitely going as planned. As planned by whom? I had no idea. I didn't plan on being this miserable. That was it. That was the whole problem.

❦

I didn't plan on anything. I just wanted to let life happen to me. Let it take me where I was intended. But was I intended to be somewhere? All I knew at that time was that I was intended to be sitting there in that bar. To drink until all memories were washed away. To do whatever it took to reboot my system. Maybe then I could go about trying to do something that would make me be whole. Because I was in shreds at the time. What an opportune time for Natalie Imbruglia to come out with Torn. Yes, that girly song really appealed to me. Because if anything, I was torn. And looking at Ms. Imbruglia in the music video, all I could think was that she looked so much like my Marya. My Marya? Yeah, right.

Chapter 65

Not only was time travel possible, it was within reach. I read a lot and somewhere I had come across the concept of time travel as one of man's God given traits. Our time machines were within us. Memories enabled us to travel to the past. Dreams made it possible to go into the future.

Yes, it was that simple. When I first read that concept, I discarded it as being another overly romanticized notion about the human condition. It wasn't until I started using my time machine that I realized how true it was. Because sitting at that train station and waiting for someone to bring me their woes in writing, all I did was some time traveling. And smoking, of course. Good thing my time machine didn't have some no smoking policy.

But there was a malfunction of sorts. I could go into the past just fine but had no way of traveling to the future. Does that mean I was some dreamless entity? Maybe. Or maybe I was just hesitant and unsure about the future because of a past that always seemed to be more haunting than memorable.

Yes, there were plenty of good memories but for some reason, the darker ones always seemed to overshadow them. And it was a sad sign that many of my fondest memories seemed to take place at Josh's Pub. No, I wasn't some alcoholic in remission. I had just had a lot of fun in that place. And, after all, I had fallen in love at that place. So what if that falling had ended up being the most miserable experience in my life. It was just the euphoria of knowing that I had achieved something so grand in the scheme of life. That is what mattered.

Yes, I was human. Damn right. I had ran the entire course of existence. So I hadn't been loved back.

Yes, that totally sucked, to put it in the coarsest manner available. But it did give me some hope. Some hope that it could happen. Some hope that it was a possibility.

Yes, hope that was utterly lost at the time when I was struck down. Even though hope just seemed like a less offensive four letter word.

Yes, me and my time machine. I hated that thing. Hated it for not letting me let go of what had been. Hated it for making me think of a possibility beyond what I had envisioned.

Then somebody came with a letter. That somebody was Marya. The Marya that was making me think of a trip to the future. Maybe the two of us would be there together. Maybe.

❦

But I lost it when she put a letter down in front of me. It had to be from her husband.

It was from her husband, that man I had started to hate. And on top of it all, she smiled as she said, " I have another one for you."

That stupid bitch, I thought. Yes, I had lost it. All attempts at holding onto what I thought I had managed to be - decent. But, as always, I lost it inside me. I hated her as she smiled and took a seat. It was all her fault. The fault of women like her. For letting themselves be pushed around. She didn't deserve this. Being hitched to a man twice her age who wasn't even around.

But she deserved it for letting it happen. All these women deserved it because they let it happen. What could she do? I don't know. Something. Anything. Take a stand. So what if they fell. They couldn't all fall. In the end, there would have to be someone left standing. And that someone could lead those who came after.

So I was a faggot since now I was thinking of female liberation. Empowering them to become something that they could.

And, well, I hated women. I hated them for letting someone like me be alone. All I had seen was the opposite sex be treated unfairly, accept the unfairness, and step over someone like me, who wanted to be so good to them.

I took the letter and opened it. I read the thing and absorbed the same old shit. And I told her what he had written - I didn't add or take anything out. Just told her what was there so she would know what her lovable hubby wanted to tell her. Nothing that was going to make her swoon or long for his return. Just the dry crap about how things were going and how he was working his ass off.

Not a word about him missing her or how he wanted to be with her. Because he didn't write any of it.

What was it with these females named Marya? Maybe if found someone with a different name, it could be different. Maybe this or maybe that. Maybe I wasn't built for this life. Maybe I was missing a part. A part that was supposed to make me more compatible for the world.

I finished the letter, folded it, put it back in the envelope, and handed it to her. She reached into her pocket book, took out a fifty rupee bill, and gave it to me. And I took it.

I honestly didn't feel like saying that she could give me whatever. No, I took the fifty, thanked her, and pulled out my pack of cigarettes.

She left.

After a couple of puffs, I started to think about whether I had acted a little rudely. I don't think I had smiled once through the entire exchange. And then there was that hateful feeling of guilt. Why did I feel guilty?

I had done all that I was supposed to do. I wasn't there to make these people happy. I was just there to let them know what was going on. That is it. These stupid people.

Maybe I needed a break. Maybe I needed another smoke. A drink was probably what I needed. But there were no bars around here. I missed Josh's Pub.

ॐ

Withdrawal. That's what it was. My body was craving something it had been deprived of for a while now. That was the only reason I could come up with for my crankiness. But, once again, I wasn't cranky on the outside. Once again, I was keeping it in me. All my life I had been afraid that one day, all that was inside me would come out. And it would be in the wrong way. I may end up becoming one of those nut jobs that went on a shooting spree. I always prayed that it would never come to such a situation. If I was going to harm anybody, it had to be myself. If I was going to be the mad gunman who went on a shooting spree and then killed himself, I hoped that I would do the later part first.

But something was majorly screwed up inside me. I still missed my Marya. Yes, MY MARYA. It didn't make sense that we would come together like we did and then just go our separate ways. No, it didn't make sense.

Was I still caught up in what I thought had been over for a long time? I guess so. There was no other way of explaining it. I thought that this job would have been helpful. Me reading and writing other people's letters. Knowing their woes and knowing that I could be worse off. It was supposed to be therapeutic. But all it did was make me feel worse. My misery was still there. Except now it was being layered with the sorrow of others. So, no, I didn't stop feeling sorry for myself. I started feeling sorry for these people as well. If anything, we all became the same. The wronged ones. Wronged by others. Wronged by fate. Wronged by beliefs. Wronged by life in general.

Chapter 66

Wasif had been my best friend at school in Islamabad. Not only were we in the same class since second grade but we also lived on the same street. Our parents had a nice setup going for us. My father used to drop us off at school in the morning and then his father would pick us up when school was over since he would get off at the same time from his job.

He worked in some factory in Rawalpindi, the city next to Islamabad. I never asked Wasif too much about what his father did and he never asked too much about mine. All that mattered was that both of us belonged to decent, hardworking families, and our parents knew each other.

It was all good.

And then I betrayed him in fifth grade.

He used to make fun of our teachers. In their absence, of course.

"Sir Faisal looks like one of those mountain goats," he would say. Sir Faisal was our Urdu teacher and he did have a beard like one of those goats. And on top of that, he was really skinny.

We would laugh and laugh.

"And that Sir Jabar is the opposite. He looks more like an ox," Wasif would go on and on.

Sir Jabar was our teacher for Islamiat, the religion class which delved deeper into how great everything was in Islam. And yes, he was a little overweight. An ox was a fitting description and we would laugh some more.

One day, Wasif and I got into a fight. Not a physical fight. Just an argument over whether or not he had given me back my game cartridge for my precious Atari 2600. He said that he had and I insisted otherwise. The argument became heated and we stopped talking to each other. We wouldn't say a single word to each other after school when his father picked us up. This went on for two days. On the third day, I found a way to get back at him since I didn't find the game - and Vanguard had been my favorite game.

I told Sir Faisal what Wasif had said about him looking like a mountain goat. And Sir Faisal had been furious. He had hit Wasif until his face had turned red from the slaps. And then Sir Faisal had taken out the dreaded cane he always kept with him. The sound echoed in the classroom as the cane was brought down on Wasif's outstretched palms.

The entire class had sat in silence because any reaction would have just diverted the wrath to whoever had made a sound.

Wasif had actually started crying. Tears were rolling down his cheeks as he was apologizing to the teacher.

Served him right for losing my favorite game, I thought as I sat and watched with the rest of the class.

When I saw him weeping, I thought that maybe it was wrong of me to have done what I had done. I was a miserable person and a lousy friend.

That was the last day my best friend Wasif talked to me.

I guess he told his parents about what had happened since after that day, our carpooling stopped and even our parents didn't mingle like they used to.

I was a miserable human.

I never found my game and actually didn't even bother to look for it after that day. It didn't matter if I found my game. I had lost my best friend and I was never going to find him again. It could never be the same.

Never.

It was just my father used to say about such things. If you cut a piece of rope in half, it could never be the same. You could tie it back together but there would always be that knot in between. Wasif and I could get back to good terms but it would never be the same. The knot would always be there.

I lost Wasif as a friend but I gained a new companion that would end up being defined as guilt.

Chapter 67

"What's up with that black box?", Jake had asked me at Ridgewood High School.

We were in ninth grade and I was nearing fifteen.

That question ended up being the one that pushed me into something I had been teetering on the edge of for quite some time.

"What black box?" I asked.

"You know, the one where all you Muslims are gathered around," he answered trying to keep his voice low since we were sitting in the library where was some kids being lectured about the Dewey Decimal System by the librarian.

"Oh, that," I said thinking of how best to explain the fifth pillar of Islam to this guy. "That is where Muslims go for their pilgrimage. They are all required to do it at least once in their life time. If they can afford it and are able to do it."

Then I went back to reading my favorite part of Reader's Digest, *Laughter, The Best Medicine.* That is all I read in that magazine. That or *All in a Day's Work, Humor in Uniform,* etc.

All the funny stuff. My parents had actually gotten a subscription the Readers Digest in Pakistan. They wanted me to learn but I just used it for entertainment.

But I guess that I did end up learning from it, anyway. Got a better grasp of the language.

"Why?" he asked.

"Well, it is the holiest place in the Muslim world. The birthplace of Islam and we were told as kids that it is the house of Allah," I said, trying to think of how best to explain it and starting to question how it didn't make sense to me. Pakistan was a Muslim country and right next to it was their worst enemy, India. What they referred to India as was Hindustan. Or land of the Hindus. And Hinduism was always told of as being the ignorant religion. A religion of many Gods when there was actually just one God, Allah. A religion made up of worshipping idols. Statues that were lifeless and couldn't do anything. How can they pray to a man made sculpture?

But isn't that the same type of thing that Muslims around the globe were doing? When Muslims prayed five times a day, they faced Mecca. Wherever in the world they were, that is the direction they faced.

So was praying to an idol any different than bowing towards a black structure, thousands of miles away?

It wasn't literally the house of Allah. It just symbolized it. But isn't that what all the idols that Hindus worshipped, signified? It wasn't like a Hindu expected the idol to move around and do anything. It was just a physical representation of their God.

And after that day, I realized that all Muslims were just worshipping a black box. Of course, if I said it out loud, I would probably be killed for that blasphemous implication.

So I never really said it out loud.

At least I kept it within me until I had a better understanding. Did I ever get that better understanding? Sure, I like to think so.

Kibla, as that holiest of places in Mecca is referred to, is the center of the Islamic world.

Hundreds of thousands go there every year for the Hajj, which is only once a year. But so many more go there all year round for the Umra which is a lesser form of the Hajj. If a Muslim has gone for the Umra, its great.

If he has gone for the Hajj, its way better. All I thought about was how much money Saudi Arabia raked in thanks to the faithful. At least, everybody was united there. Back home in Pakistan, I saw Shias hating the Sunnis and vice versa.

I was from a Sunni family and of course they were the right branch. Unfortunately, one of my very good friends in school, Hassan, was a Shia. Everything was good until the realization in my young mind that if the Sunnis were right, it meant that Hassan's family were wrong. And that meant he would go to hell. There was no other way around it. My family and I were going to heaven while he and his family were hell bound. I must have been around eight at the time and I spent many nights crying in bed and praying to Allah to show Hassan and his family the right path.

But I digress. The point is that to me, it all came down to being about having faith in something more powerful than ourselves. I had no idea how to explain the world or what was going on in it. So I just decided to step away from Islam, take all that I had been taught, filter out what I deemed unnecessary, and live my life with a hope that whoever God was would have a better understanding of what I had chosen.

Of course, in the eyes of the elders, I was hell bound. And what bothered them more was the fact that I took it so easy.

"Heaven," I would say, "sounds a little boring since from the looks of it, I will know more people down there than up there."

Heads were shaken and prayers were said for my guidance.

Thank you for the concern, I just said. Then I read No Exit from Sartre. And then I met Marya Durani. And it started to make sense.

Yes, hell is other people.

Chapter 68

Life was good.

Once.

Did I screw it up for myself or was a greater power behind it?

Now that was a tough spot for me to be in. I think I cornered myself with that bit. Yes, I was a big believer in God. Remember, I became an agnostic and not an atheist.

So with my faith came the belief that the good Lord hadn't set out to leave us screwed.

No.

We had free will. We were not puppets with our every action predestined. We were given our choice in the matter. But what bothered me was the fact that when the choices came, we didn't really have too much to get us out of our cornered position.

Yes, I did believe in fate. That there was a certain place we were going to end up. And this is the part that made me feel I was getting screwed. If I was meant to be someone in a certain place, did it matter what I chose in life since I was going to end up there one way or another. If there was such a thing as fate then what good was trying to fight something that would just make the journey to my predestined situation more difficult. I could just sit there, do nothing, and still end up where I was meant to end up.

Was I just meant to end up sitting there and doing nothing?

It didn't bother me. A better way of putting it would be that it annoyed the hell out of me.

Would it have been easier if I had just gone to live with Taya Ji and taken over for his letter writing? If I had not gone through the whole gauntlet of going to the US, living there, falling, getting my heart shattered, and then come to him.

No, I liked to think that I was not meant to travel in a straight line. I was meant to have gone the way that I had to end up back in the country I was born in. I liked to think of it as my destiny calling.

"Hello," a quiet sounding voice brought me out of my stupor.

"Hi," I said opening my eyes and seeing what I had been hoping to see. It was Marya with a letter that seemed to have gone through the postal systems of the entire globe before coming into her possession.

She had the same dress I had seen her in most of the times. A light beige colored shalwar kameez with a brown dupata thrown over her shoulders. A shalwar was pretty much like pants except that it was a lot looser. The culture and religion didn't want the women dressed in any fashion that would be too close to their physical contours. Same thing with the kameez – just like a shirt but looser and coming down to the knees. Of course, the way she was wearing the dupata was something that would be considered obscene by the devout.

The dupatas were the thin sheets that were supposed to cover the women's hair. She just had it slung over her shoulders. Covering the hair was very important since that is what was supposed to define a woman's beauty. The belief was that if a woman's hair was thoroughly covered, you couldn't really judge her looks. In my opinion, women who covered their heads and faces thoroughly, only drew more stares from the gawking males by arousing their curiosity.

But that was me.

"Another letter," I said reaching for the envelope in her outstretched hand.

She just nodded her shy nod and sat down in the chair that I kept thinking about replacing with one in better shape. After all, I didn't want the thing breaking on one of my clients.

Yes, my clients. I say it as if I was running some big corporate office catering to the spoiled. But to me these were my clients. Broke, broken, and without much hope of getting out of a rut that they had been born into. Yes, my clients. My people.

The envelope was already open. I think she probably opened it to just look at the words written on the piece of paper inside. Maybe it made her feel closer to her husband… touching that piece of paper that he had touched and written on. Or maybe I was overly romantic in my head.

I always gave the letters a quick scan. Tried to get the gist of the material at hand before I started reading it to the people. Maybe it was my way of being cautious in case some improvisation was going to be needed.

And this letter wasn't good news. It wasn't bad news for her. But it wasn't good news to me. Her husband was coming back to Pakistan.

Chapter 69

I loved working at the Patel's little convenience store. It was my school.

Actually, it was better than school. I think I'd gotten more life experience there than I had at Ridgewood High School. So everyday I would start off at my school there and then graduate to Josh's Pub every night.

I would think almost every day about how my parents would be so disappointed,. But it was okay since I was going to make them proud eventually. How? I had no damn idea.

I read a lot, when business was slow which it was a lot of times. I usually went through all the newspapers. They got around five or six different papers. The Daily News, NY Post, NY Times, Home News and Tribune, and some local papers about the town.

Yes, I went through them all. I wasn't too crazy about the Times because I always said that it was a little too snooty for not having comics.

Because that was my favorite part of the paper… the comics. Or the movie section.

I could actually go through the movie section without any fear. Fear? Yes, because back in Pakistan, I was absolutely forbidden to go through the movie section in the newspaper.

We used to get the Daily Jang delivered to our house in Pakistan. I guess it was like the NY Times over there. Just that Jang means war in Urdu.

Gives you a little impression about the culture, I guess. Having a newspaper with such violent implications in its title. There were no comics in there but it did have ads for movies playing in the local cinemas. I just loved looking at the pictures advertising those movies. Of course, those pictures were altered from their original state. Remember that this was a Muslim country so there couldn't be any pictures of scantily clad women. Guns were okay but no cleavages or legs showing.

So how were these pictures altered? If there was a female with a short skirt on then the legs were painted black to make it look like she had pants on or something like that.

Seriously, I am not kidding. I never went to the cinema there so I have no idea how those movies played on the big screen.

But if my father ever caught me looking at the movie section in the newspaper, I was in big trouble. Movies were bad. Books were good. Especially encyclopedias and other stuff that I found boring as hell.

Heck, we didn't get a VCR until I was eight or so and even then, it just sat there under the TV. I think my dad would let me rent a movie once every two weeks. We would go to the video rental store and he would ask for some "family" movie that was going to be appropriate for me. That meant no sex or nudity. Blood and guts, sure. But no sex or nudity.

That is how I was raised. And I will never hold it against my parents for doing what they thought was best for me.

But if they were trying to give me this sheltered existence, then why take away the cover so abruptly? Send me off to the US which was everything I didn't know. It could have been done a little slowly. I could have been eased into adulthood. But they just pushed me into the deep end of the pool without any knowledge of what to do. Now it does sound like I was holding it against them, doesn't it? No, I am not holding my upbringing against them. I am just a little resentful about being sent to the US and being expected to do everything that just seemed unnatural for a person my age. They had given me a compass but I felt like I needed a map. Which is how I started to look at religion when I got around to shunning it. As a compass. Something that was good for pointing out the rights and wrongs. But not something to be adhered to like a map.

Yes, that was it. I got it. But all these stupid people didn't seem to grasp the simplicity of God's plan. It was amazing how brilliant I was. No, actually I was a retard when it came to life. A stupid shit head without a clue who had decided to abandon his map for a compass that was broken.

Chapter 70

What aggravated me the most was the knowledge that I was miserable over someone I had never had. Someone who had been part of my life for less than a week and left me in tatters. Okay, so this is what love was supposed to be like. Fine. I would go along with it. But it was supposed to get better. Right? I mean, how could my pure and honest intentions be scorned by fate. God couldn't possibly want someone like me to be where I was now. Maybe there was no God. Maybe when I abandoned religion for agnosticism, I should have also abandoned any faith in an Almighty.

I thought so. And I hated myself for thinking so. I went around with a constant prayer in my head asking for forgiveness for thinking what I had thought. I talked to God in my head and I asked for forgiveness. And I asked for guidance. And I asked for some enlightenment. And then I felt guilty over all my asking. It seemed so selfish. So I asked God for the ability to do what I needed to do to be a better person. I figured that would make up for my selfishness in asking for all that I did.

But then I thought about it and realized that I was still looking out for myself. So I abandoned that. After all, Marya didn't choose me.

Fine. So I asked God to give her happiness with the choice she had made. Maybe it was better. Somehow.

That's when I had started to feel a little better. A little less miserable. Was this what it meant to be over someone?

I guess it had to be it. I was over Marya Durani. But I would be a damn liar if I said that I didn't miss her.

I don't think I can define it as something that aggravated me, though. I think it was more something that pissed me off… I was angry at myself for believing that I needed her.

I didn't need her.

Then why was I constantly thinking of her? Why did I want her to be there with me? What the hell was wrong with me?

❦

I am sure that if I confided in any of my elders about my situation, they would just tell me that I should return to Islam. Do as the Koran says and I could be at peace with myself and the world around me. It was the way. It was the *light*.

Maybe they have it right. Was it pride that was getting in the way? The stubbornness of not admitting that maybe I had been wrong. Maybe being a devout Muslim would have been the smart way of going through life. Yes, I knew that I could achieve some control over my inner turmoil if I just followed blindly. But the only problem with that was that after having questioned the faith, I couldn't just return to it without having gotten some sort of answers. Even if I ended up becoming a devoted Muslim, I knew that I was returning to it because I had failed to achieve any answers on my own.

I would know that I had failed and I didn't want that.

What pissed me off even more was the synchronicity of everything. Maybe Allah had sent Marya my way to show me how wrong I was. All I knew was that I didn't know anything.

God knows I had always had the right intentions. The purest intentions, if I dare say.

I was going to help Taya Ji and that was going to help me. Once again, I was doing something self less with the most selfish of intentions. I was only helping him because I had nowhere to turn to. No place in this world.

Should I go back to my parents? Then how the hell was I going to explain myself? I had always thought that I had had a good relationship with them. But it wasn't until now that I realized it had been a facade.

I had only done what they had expected me to do. I loved them but hated the fact that I could never approach them with my inner most problems. Once again, there was the religious aspect. They had shown me the path and if I had just stuck to it, there wouldn't be any complications. But one thing they hadn't prepared me for was what to do in case questions did arise. How the hell was I going to get around the hurdles if my inquiries remained unanswered?

I was in such deep shit.

ੴ

And thinking about all this wasn't helping. But I had nothing else to do. I think it could be easily said that I had cornered myself. It was all my fault. God didn't do this. I did.

I had been a believer in free will. And this was all the doing of my own free will. I still tried to find my way out of it so I wouldn't get the blame. Sure, everyone had free will. But I had no choice in where I got to use it. If I was put in a situation where all of my choices seemed to be heading nowhere, then I couldn't be blamed. I always felt like I had come to an intersection where all roads were one way streets and I couldn't turn anywhere. The only two way street was the one I had just come down. I could turn around and go back but that was not possible in life. I couldn't go back.

Yes, I was in deep shit.

ੴ

Then somebody came with a letter. Thank God. It was only the second person in the past four hours. And it was the same bullshit. See, I was so fed up with it all that I was looking at this poor old man's troubles as bullshit.

But, honest to God, it was the same bullshit. Son is in Qatar and is writing about how he misses the family and wants to see them. It is such hard work in Qatar and the boss won't give him any time off to come and visit the family.

And all the father wants me to write to him is if he can send home some money since things are so bad financially. I guess that it is their only son. I just guess and don't ask any further because I don't care. Maybe a part of me cares but part of me wants to just get the job over with and send the old man on his way.

The later part wins.

I took the fifty rupees from the old man and said Khuda Hafiz to his departing words of Allah Hafiz. Yes, the battle between my Khuda and his Allah rages on.

Whoever wins, I seem to lose.

Chapter 71

Okay, now bear with me on this. I know it is probably annoying by now but Marya Durani was really meant to be with me.

I mean, what are the chances of someone like me falling for someone like her? Sure, it doesn't seem that far fetched but keep in mind that I was in the US. I was supposed to be dodging these sirens that supposedly loomed all around and tempted poor innocent Pakistanis like me.

Hey, I am sorry but that's what I was told by the elders. Stupid elders. So I meet this Pakistani girl and I fall in love with her. Doesn't that strike you as being fate?

No? Forget it. Let me move on.

Lying on the floor at Taya Ji's, I thought about what I should do. Or what I shouldn't do. Should I go back to my parents? Ami knew I was back. Had she told Abu? Should I go see my father, at least? It wouldn't be pleasant but I don't think he deserved to be ignorant of his only son's whereabouts.

The poor man probably thought that I was getting a super education in America and that I would be coming back with my degree in business administration.

Yes, along the way, we had eventually compromised. He had told me that there were only three careers worth pursuing. I could be a lawyer. I could get an MBA. Or I could be a doctor. Becoming a doctor was the best choice for me since one didn't have to be too sharp to be a doctor. Yes, those were his exact words. I wasn't sharp enough to be a lawyer or get an MBA.

I was smart. Just not sharp. So I should be a doctor.

It had taken a lot of forcing but I talked him out of seeing me as a doctor. I would like to get an MBA, I had asked him. He wasn't too sure but had finally agreed.

Sure, if that is what I wanted then I should go for that. So my field of forced options had gotten down to me getting an MBA.

Did I want to? Hell, no.

I was just trying to buy myself some time. Some time until what? I had no damn idea.

What was going to happen? Well, I wanted to do something that would make me useful to humanity. Yes, that is how idealistic I was. Maybe I could be a social worker.

One of my heroes, while growing up in Pakistan, had been Abdul Sattar Edhi. He was a man dedicated to serving his fellow man. He ran his charitable organization, composed of orphanages and facilities for free healthcare for the needy. The old timer did so much for his fellow country men and asked for nothing in return. Now that is what a true Muslim should be like. Not one spending his days praying for a blessed afterlife but one who would make this life better for his fellow man.

Did I mention I was idealistic? Parents in Pakistan didn't raise their kids to become social workers. They wanted doctors, lawyers, or businessmen.

So I was screwed by the society. And in all this commotion over what I was going to be, I had lost track of what I was becoming.

I was becoming nothing. A delusional, romantic, nobody.

But God was going to show me the way. That is what I believed. That is what I had hoped for.

Then I heard the Fajr azaan coming from the speakers of the mosque by Taya Ji's shack. Fajr was the first prayer of the day. It was at the crack of dawn and was meant to get the Muslims started on their day.

Damn, did this mean that I had just lied awake all night? It was going to be a rough day.

Taya Ji stepped out of his bed, trying not to make too much noise since the bed was in pretty bad condition and there was the constant squeaking. The thing was going to fall apart any day which is why

I actually felt safer sleeping on the floor. At least I didn't have far to fall.

Once again, my intent was a little deceptive. Did I give him the higher plane to rest on out of respect or was I just looking out for myself? The thing was in bad shape though. Four wooden posts held together by rope which also doubled as the surface on which one slept. No mattress. Just the luxury of a pillow which looked like it had been trampled on by a herd of elephants.

He stepped around me quietly since I had always had this habit of sleeping on my stomach with my face buried in my pillow. The pillows had been nice and plump once. Now it was just a pillow cover stuffed with some foamy material.

Hey, it was better than resting my head on the solid and hard floor.

Taya Ji went to the bathroom and I just laid there with my eyes closed. Yes, it was going to be a rough day since I already felt tired.

And then I heard a loud crash come from the bathroom. I sat straight up and looked around.

"Taya Ji," I said in a loud voice but there was no response.

I got up and went to the bathroom. Thank God, he hadn't locked it from inside. I opened the door just a bit to get a peak inside and saw his legs on the floor. No motion.

I pushed the door open and stepped inside.

He was lying on the floor.

I rushed over to his side and squatted down on the floor. He wasn't breathing and was completely motionless.

"Taya Ji," I said lifting his head off the floor. I looked at my hand and there was blood. He must have hit his head on the floor when he fell. Was he unconscious because he had hit his head on the floor or had he hit his head after falling from a lack of consciousness.

I had no idea and I tried to calm myself.

I got up, looked around, and tried not to panic since it was too late for that.

I didn't need to be a doctor to know that he was gone.

Taya Ji was dead.

Chapter 72

I used to think about people around me dying. God forbid, I didn't want people around me dying. I used to just think about how I would react to someone dying. Would I be happy if someone I didn't like died? I hoped not. Would I cry if someone close to me died? I had no idea.

My grandmother had died when I was around seven years old. It was my mother's mom and my mom had been a wreck. She was crying uncontrollably and kept looking at me to see how I was doing. I, honest to God, had no urge to shed a tear. But I did cry. Not for my grandmother. I cried because my mother was sad.

My mother had hugged me and kept on telling me that it was okay. In my heart I knew it was okay. My grandma, or "nani" as I called her, was over seventy years old. I thought she had lived a good life. I thought it was very cold of me to think so, but even at the age of seven, I didn't see it as a total loss.

Nani had lived her life. She had served her purpose. She had raised her kids well and seen them reach their goals. Yes, I was seven and I was thinking about this stuff. I wasn't sad. It was just seeing my mother bawling uncontrollably that made me sad. I loved my nani and I was going to miss her. But there just wasn't any urge to cry. Just that artificial need to shed a few tears so others wouldn't categorize me as being the cold hearted grandson.

Falling off of my bike as a kid and hurting myself had made me cry. Those were true tears. But nani's death had only resulted in a tearful facade.

Sad movies made me cry. But why the hell didn't I cry at nani's funeral?

And now I sat on the bathroom floor cradling taya ji's head and without an inkling of how exactly to feel.

I was going to miss the old man. Actually, I missed him already. But I couldn't cry. And then the most loathsome feeling overcame me as I felt a tear roll down my cheek. I was crying but it wasn't for taya ji.

I was crying because I was lost. What the hell was I going to do now? I couldn't possibly go back to my parents because my father was going to give me hell.

Was I afraid?

I wasn't afraid of confronting him. I was just afraid of facing him as a disappointment. A disappointment of everything he had wanted me to be.

I just leaned my head against the cold wall and closed my eyes. And then I thought.

If things had worked out with Marya Durani, everything would have been okay. It was all that bitch's fault.

And then I corrected myself. It wasn't her fault. It was all my fault. What did any of what I was thinking have to do with what was going on right now? Taya Ji's body was laying by my feet. I should do something.

It would have been so easy in the US. I would have just dialed 911 and all the assistance I needed would have been there. But this wouldn't have happened in the US. No. This shit was only happening to me in this third world country. Who do I call? There wasn't even a phone in this shack that I had started calling home. Where was a nearby hospital? Or wherever they handled this kind of stuff. All I knew about was Holy Family Hospital somewhere in Rawalpindi. That's where I was born. Other than that I had no knowledge of any hospitals around there.

But would I need to get in touch with a hospital? There wasn't anything they could do.

I finally decided to get off the floor and go outside to ask someone for help. I got up, went outside, and lit a cigarette. Yes, that's what I needed. It was going to calm me down.

Three cigarettes later, I was still a wreck. I finally decided to go to the shop around the corner and use their phone. To call whom? I decided to call my parents. I hoped my mother would answer but realized I may actually have to talk to my father if he was the one to answer.

I gave the guy a couple of ten rupee bills and started to dial the number. God help me is all I could think.

Actually, divine help was something that got shoved aside as a realization entered my mind while I was dialing the number. That realization came with a side car loaded with guilt.

Whenever Taya Ji woke up in the morning, he would wake me up as well. To give me some time to get ready for my day at the station. But he didn't do it that morning. Was he angry at me? Was he holding that argument we had the night before against me?

Oh yes, the argument. A friendly discussion that got a little heated.

"So you don't believe in Islam?" he asked me.

"Well," I began a little hesitatingly since I didn't want to say anything that would offend him. He was a strict believer. He just wasn't running off to the mosque or following the mullahs as enthusiastically as those feigning a devotion that wasn't entirely there. And I respected that. He didn't do anything for show. He believed and just couldn't get himself to follow what Islam had become. A mosque on every corner resulting in more divisiveness than unity.

"I just can't see how the things from so long ago can still be relevant. Maybe a little change since times have changed," I said. Then added, "a lot."

That wasn't a good call on my part which I realized as he put down his cup of tea and looked at me with eyes that I had never seen so filled with anger.

But he didn't raise his voice.

"So you think it should be like those Christians do it? Keep changing God's will to suit them," he said in a stern tone. "Well, Mohammed was the last of his prophets and whatever message came through him, it was the last one. Do you know how many prophets there were?"

"Yes, one hundred and twenty four thousand," I said. I think that actually may have impressed him since there was a glimmer of a smile on his face. At least I thought so.

"Yes, and Mohammed was the last one. Our last chance at correcting our ways," he said.

And then I said something that I shouldn't have said. Or something I could have phrased better.

"Maybe Allah, as you guys call him, should rethink things a little and send another prophet. You know, seeing how things haven't really turned out as he may have intended."

That was it. He put down the cup of tea with such force that I was afraid it may actually get cracked.

And then he didn't say a single word. He went to the bathroom, came out and went to bed.

As I laid down on the floor, I said "Khuda hafiz," in a quiet voice. He didn't say anything in response. Maybe he didn't hear me.

I wasn't going to find out. He was angry at me when he died.

I was a miserable human being.

The sound of the bell ringing on the other end of the line made me realize I was done dialing the number.

"Hello," a male voice answered ending my stupor. Great, I thought, knowing it was time to talk to my father. It had been a while.

Chapter 73

Maybe it wasn't time to talk to my father. That must be why I opened my mouth to say something and decided to hang up, because nothing came out.

"Nobody is there," I said to the guy behind the counter who had been busy watching the cricket game he had on the little Toshiba TV he had behind the counter.

"Oh," he said turning around with a look of disappointment since he would have to give me my money back.

"I will try some other time," I said as I started to walk towards the door without any mention of a refund.

"Here," he said putting my money on the counter.

I just took one of the ten rupee bills and told him to keep the other for his trouble. There wasn't any trouble but I knew that the call had gone through and he would be charged. I had no idea how much that charge would be but figured that the ten would be sufficient.

He thanked me and went back to watching his game… That was something I had never been into. Watching sports, that is.

In the US, I had been pretty blunt when I told people the only sport I liked to watch was the Super Bowl and that was just for the commercials.

I walked out of the shop, stood outside for a while, looked around for a while, and realized what was missing. Yes, I wasn't smoking. So I pulled out a cigarette, lit it, and started walking back to Taya Ji's.

What the hell was I going to do now, I thought. I had no idea.

It would definitely not be like the US where all the authorities needed to be summoned in case of someone dying. The cops, the paramedics, and God knows who else.

I decided to go to the local mosque. The only problem was having to decide which one to go to since there were around three in the neighborhood of his place. I just decided to go to the one that seemed the closest.

It was empty at the time since it was too early for the Zohr, or afternoon prayers.

I took off my shoes but kept the socks on since I was pretty sure that was okay.

"Can I help you?" a voice said as my eyes were wandering around the empty hall for any signs of life.

"Yes," I said, noticing the maulwi dressed in a white shalwar kameez emerge from the side of the building.

Actually, describing the mosque as a building may conjure up images of grandeur. But, no, it was a small building. Probably thirty or forty men managed to squeak in there for the Friday prayers; Friday, the holiest day of the week.

"My Taya Ji passed away this morning," I said looking at the maulwi with a downward gaze since it was a little embarrassing to be standing there in my ragged jeans, flannel shirt, and a pierced ear. No, I didn't feel guilty about my appearance. I was just respectful of what others may conceive as improper.

"I am sorry," he said after reciting a prayer in Arabic which was said whenever someone's passing was mentioned. That was actually one of the things in Islam that I had liked. The prayer which meant "from him we come and to him we shall return."

"And he doesn't have anyone else around here," I said. "I was just visiting him when it happened."

I hoped that the maulwi sahib wouldn't ask too many questions. The maulwi's were the caretakers of the mosques. They were the ones who were responsible for the calls to prayer, or azaans, five times a day; also then they were the ones who led the prayer. If this was anything like the mosque that had been by the house where I had grown up then his living quarters were probably attached to the mosque as well.

It was a voluntary job since there wasn't someone in management to give a monthly paycheck. But the people around the neighborhood probably gave him some sort of monetary compensation.

Plus there was the school, or madrasa, where he would teach the kids after their school. That is teach them about Islam and supervise their reading of the Koran. Whatever the children's parents compensated him also added to his salary. That is how things worked. At least that is how it had been when I was growing up.

"We must get the body ready and have his namaaz-e-janazaa with the Zohr prayers in the afternoon," he said.

Yes, there were no fancy preparations for a burial in Islam. No suit and no coffin. The body was given a bath, then there was a prayer where all the males would say their prayers with the body before them. However that was the only prayer where there was no bowing, like in the rest of the prayer. You only bowed to Allah and bowing to the body lying in front of you was a no-no.

Then the body would be wrapped in a white sheet and buried without a coffin so it would become one with the earth as soon as possible.

Coffins would delay that procedure.

And that was another aspect of Islam that I liked. To have a person's body become one with the ground it was buried in.

In the US, there had to be a coffin. So Muslims over there would give their loved ones the cheapest possible coffin. It wasn't thriftiness. It was just their way of finding some way to respect the law while not being disrespectful to their faith. But the burial had to be done as soon as possible after the demise.

"Okay, then," he said, "take me to him and we will start preparing."

He shouted some names towards the back of the mosque and a couple of young guys came running after a short while. He explained the situation to them and we all went back to Taya Ji's.

Thank God, nothing was said on the way back.

Actually, I think it would have been better if we had been talking. Then, maybe, I wouldn't be thinking about the hole I was in.

Chapter 74

It started to pour.

❦

When I was in Mrs. Miller's ninth grade Honors English class at Ridgewood High School, she told us never to use clichés in our writing assignments. Phrases that were hackneyed were a big "no-no."

I don't think I ever did that. Sure, in the beginning, I made a few mistakes but eventually I learned. But my whole case was with what was so bad about using a cliché now and then. After all, I thought that a statement reached a clichéd status after having been around a while. Maybe it was used so often because there was some truth to it. Try explaining that to an English teacher in her sixties who was living a solitary life where picking on the students counted as a social activity.

So I tried not to use clichés. A penny was never earned when one was saved and it never rained cats and dogs.

But I have no other way of describing what was happening to me. Bad fortune had literally been pouring on me.

When it rains it pours, they say.

It could go either way, couldn't it? Why couldn't good things pour like the unfortunate ones?

I had no answer for that.

First, I had lost Marya Durani. Yes, it is possible to lose something you have never had to begin with. But I tried to get around that by blaming myself. It wasn't her fault.

Then I had tried to start over in Pakistan. There I had lost Marya Sajid. Fine, I was happy for her. Happy that her husband was coming back. I was still in the process of trying to figure out what I would do if he got around to realize that she believed he had written things that he hadn't. What would I do? But then Taya Ji died.

Yes, it was pouring.

I went to his namaaz e janazaa, or funeral prayers but I didn't do a single thing. I just stood there with my arms folded in front of me. There were about fifteen other people there. I didn't know any of them. They had just come for the zohr, or afternoon prayers and had stayed when maulwi sahib had told them about the passing of their dear comrade. I doubt that they knew Taya Ji, but they had stayed because they probably saw it as extra credit.

After the prayers, they had offered me their condolences and then lifted the wooden plank which held Tays Ji's body. Four of us had carried the body to the nearby graveyard, and buried him. The grave digger was an old fellow who didn't seem too far from joining the ranks of his clients. I gave him a fifty rupee bill and thanked him.

He offered his condolences and wanted to know if there were any other kids besides me.

No kids, I explained. I was just a nephew.

When I came back to the shack that we had called home, I actually cried.

Poor Taya Ji, I thought. This had been his whole life. And he had nobody else to remember him.

Maybe I should have told my father. But if my father cared, he wouldn't have let his brother be alone like he had been.

What to do? I had no idea.

Sit, think, smoke, think, and smoke some more.

And for some odd reason, the thought that came to my mind was regarding when I was eight years old. Our next door neighbors were Mr. and Mrs. Mirza. They had two daughters and the older one was my age. Saima, was her name and we had been friends since before we could talk. When she had turned eight, they had thrown her a birthday party. All her friends were invited and I was the only boy there.

I was over at their house the day before the party and we were discussing which games to play. They had this one game where a ball was passed around while the tape recorder played music. Then, one of the parents would stop the tape and the passing of the ball would stop. Whoever had the ball at the time would reach into the bowl in the center and pull out a slip of paper from the ones that filled the bowl. Then they would have to do whatever the paper said.

"Dance on one leg," said Myra, one of the other friends that was there.

Sure, everyone agreed and it was added.

"How about, kiss the person to your left on the cheek?" Saima said as she wrote it down.

Yes, yes, everyone agreed.

And then it hit me. What if I got that? It meant I would have to kiss one of the girls since I was going to be the only guy there.

There was no way in hell that was going to happen. Because that was the society I had been raised in. Boys and girls were kept separate.

Just my luck that my neighbors had to have two daughters. I grew up with them and it was the only reason we were allowed to be around each other.

So my quest began to try to convince Saima's parents to invite Javed from across the street. He was around our age and an only child.

The parents finally agreed. Javed was invited, the birthday party began, and I made sure he sat to my left when we got around to playing that game. Of course the music stopped when I had the ball and, of course, I pulled out the slip of paper that ordered me to kiss the person to my left.

Thank God, I thought, that Javed was to my left. I gave him a quick peck on the cheek and it was over.

That was the society I was raised in. Men were allowed to have three wives but boys weren't supposed to talk to girls.

It was strange but what was even stranger was the fact that this thought had entered my mind.

Chapter 75

"Can I smoke?" I asked the taxi driver.

"Sure, sir," he replied with a smile while looking in his rearview mirror.

"Don't ever call me sir," I said as I pulled out my pack of cigarettes, lit one, and rolled down the window just a crack.

I hated being called "sir." Not because it made me feel older than I was but because I felt too much pressure from that small three letter word. I didn't deserve to be called "sir." I didn't feel I was worthy of being called that.

If only this guy knew me. He would never call me that. And he was older than me. Must have been in his forties. When someone older called me "sir," not only did I feel unworthy but I also felt guilty. Guilty for being in a position where someone who shouldn't have to call me that, felt the need to call me that, just to get something from me. If it was to get something, than it was even worse.

Nobody should have to stoop to that level. If it was rightfully theirs than I should give it to them without being asked. If it wasn't then they could pull out my fingernails and I still wouldn't give it. That's the kind of stubborn person I was.

So I smoked my cigarette and felt that most pleasant of feelings whenever I took a drag. No, not the smoke going in me but the mixture of the cool air from outside mix with the minimal amount of heat generated when the cigarette was so close to my face.

Yes, that felt good.

That was the only thing that felt good.

I had given up. Actually, I think it felt better to say that I had surrendered. I was going to my parents.

Yes, life had won. I was going back to mommy and daddy. It felt just like when I had been around seven years old. I had fallen off my bike and scraped my knee on the road. I came running home with tears rolling down my face. Mom had hugged me, kissed me, and sat me down on the chair to put bandages on my knees. Yes, it was a little like that.

Just that I wasn't going to be crying and there wasn't anything that my mother could do to ease the pain.

I had packed all of taya ji's belongings in a small bag. He didn't have much, so it was easy. What I did come across when going through his closet was an old photo album with black and white pictures of him as a child. I think it was him. Or it could be my father. Or it could be my other uncle in the US. But there was only one picture with all three of them. Couldn't tell who was who but I just knew that it was all three of them. All three of them with my dada and dadi. Or grandpa and grandma if it feels easier for you.

I looked out the window and saw the cars passing by.

Or maybe it was us passing them by. Who knows?

I thought about Marya. My first love. I hoped she was happy. Then I thought about Marya Sajid. And I hoped her husband was good to her upon his return. And I thought of all the people who had come to me with their woes, joys, and issues. I hoped they would be okay without me.

But who the hell was I to think that they needed me? They didn't need me. They would be fine without me. God bless them, I thought. God bless everyone.

Should I have told the station master that I wouldn't be setting up my table any longer? Nah, he'd figure something out sooner or later.

"Here we are, sir," the driver said pulling in front of the house where I had grown up.

"Sir? Again?," I said in an angry tone and then gave the guy a smile to let him know it was all good.

He went to the back, opened the trunk and took out the two suitcase that weren't fitting up front with me.

I took all my stuff, paid him, thanked him, and walked up to the gate.

Should I be doing this, I thought. I didn't know. I would never know. I rang the bell hoping that it wasn't too late. It was only nine o clock but it got dark early in the winter and my parents used to go to bed early. At least when I had been with them.

The door opened and I saw my father looking out. I was still at the outside gate by the end of the driveway. He stepped out and started walking towards the gate. Did he recognize me? Had mom told him about my return or had she kept the secret?

"Irfan?" he said as he opened the outside door.

"Yes, sir," I replied.

This was going to be hard.

"Who is it?" my mother asked as she came out too.

I gave my father a hug. But it was when I gave my mother a hug that I realized something.

I was crying.

Epilogue

"How is it?," ami asked as she showed me to my room.

She didn't need to show me to my room. I had been gone a while but I could have found it blindfolded.

"Its good," I said with a smile.

"Okay, now take a little rest and we will do the catching up tomorrow," she said as she left the room and closed the door behind her.

It was going to be okay, I said to myself as I laid back on my twin sized bed. It was 9:30 at night and I think it was a Tuesday. I am not really sure.

I looked around my room and found it to be just as I had left it. Ami had taken good care of it. She probably had the cleaning lady go over the vacant part of the house just as she would over the occupied area.

The walls were still the light blue color I had left them. They had to have had it repainted while I was gone.

My Knight Rider poster was still on the wall. I had been a big fan of the show even though as I had gotten older, I had turned my back on it. I had started to label it as being stupid and immature. But I had always kept that poster on the wall.

I couldn't turn my back on who I had been.

So there was Michael Knight standing by a gleaming KITT and flashing me a smile. But in the corner of the room were my most prized possessions.

All my stuffed toys sitting on the floor just as I had left them. Bugs Bunny, Mickey Mouse, Boris, Natasha, and some generic teddy bears.

Just as I had left them. My loyal buddies. They would never give up on me.

I looked at the walls and remembered my artistic side. When we had first moved into the place, I had been two years old. My father had spent all of the money on building the house. There hadn't been enough left to paint the interior or the exterior. I didn't care because ami and abu had given me chalk to keep me busy. And all day, I would draw on those bare walls. Cats, dogs, or whatever came to my two-year-old mentality. Yes, I was a budding artist.

And my parents had been so proud of the nonsensical figures that I drew on the walls.

They would show them to their friends with pride.

"Irfan looks like he is going to be an artist," they would say.

Nobody knew of the nothing that was in the making.

I heard thunder outside as the rain started to fall.

Should I, I thought to myself. No, it was time to rest. But I was going to try it again.

Find the end of the rain.

I must have been around ten when I became obsessed with finding the end of rain. It had to be there. It didn't rain all over the world at the same time. There had to be that place where rain stopped. Where one step would take you into dryness. I just wanted to find that place where rain stopped.

So I could just jump back and forth between rain and absolute dryness.

It rained quite often in Islamabad. I would get my chance again.

And God willing, I was going to find that place. And then I would stand there, half dry and half soaked.

Someday...

Second Epilogue

They always said that one's life flashes before their eyes when they have a near death experience.

I had a few of those moments. No, not near death experiences. Just instances when my life flashed before my eyes. Maybe its because my life didn't amount to much. So there were times when I would just see everything that I had gone through. Those I had loved. the few that I hated, and the few that might have been. Might have been what? I had no idea.

But the one time in my life that I had expected to see the entirety of my existence, there had been just a casual ennui, accompanied by nothing.

No signs of the past and no hopes for the future.

I was behind the counter at the Patel's. Just me. A guy walked in and went to the Pepsi fridge and brought his can of Mug Root Beer to the counter. With tax, it came to eighty six cents. He gave me a dollar and I gave him fifteen cents back since I was too lazy to count

out four pennies.

"Thanks," I said and his response was pulling out a gun. Some gray revolver type thing. Was it real? Only one way of finding out and I didn't care to go to that extreme.

"Empty the register," he said.

I didn't do anything since I was a little taken back by this genuinely new experience. He just reached over the counter and into the open register since I didn't seem to be up to his demand. He took out all the bills and even the tray that held the change.

"Empty out the lottery," he said, pointing the gun to the other side of the counter where a lottery machine should have been.

"Do you see a fucking lottery machine there?," I said in a blunt tone while staying seated in the chair.

"You don't have lotto?" he said.

I didn't even respond. Just rolled my eyes. It was taking too long and luckily for him, no customers had come in. He just stuffed the cash in his pocket, grabbed the change drawer and started heading out the door.

"Can you leave the change drawer?" I said.

He looked at me, not believing what he had heard. After all, I had just asked a man brandishing a gun to give me back the change.

I had managed to stay perfectly calm. Why? Because I was calm. I had a gun shoved in my face and all I had thought about was someone coming in, spending a quarter, giving me a dollar, and me not having any change to give back.

The guy put the change drawer down on the counter and walked out the door, making sure not to appear like he was fleeing the scene.

I put the change back in the register, picked up the phone, and dialed 911.

I hadn't even broken a sweat.

When I thought about it later on, I realized that I had just had a near death experience. But why the hell hadn't my life flashed before my eyes? Maybe I knew I wasn't going to die like this.

No, I was meant to suffer through life without having an easy way out.

Acknowledgements

The story I set out to tell is over. What is this then? I am not sure what to call it. Acknowledgements? Thank you's? I like the second one better. So these are my thank you's. Please don't stop reading now. At least give the people, who made this possible, credit by reading on. Thank God this is not one of those award acceptance speeches where the orchestra starts playing its music to make the recipient know that they have gone on too long and must hurry up. So in no particular order here are my thank you's. Thank you to all my friends. Matt Kokotowski for not letting me be the straight arrow I was meant to be. For showing me how to be a little unsafe. For introducing me to a little wilder side of life. But I still insist that you failed in your goal to see me hammered. Craig Cheng for being the straight arrow that my mom had hoped I would be.

Emiliano Martinez for opening my eyes to some cinema I would never have known if you hadn't forced me to watch those so called "classics." I still think you over rated Ringo Lam as a director and Chow Yun Fat as an actor. Thanks to all my buddies at RBs. Thanks Frankie and Chris for serving me even though you knew I wasn't twenty one. Thank you Fred Siebert, Walter Sosnowski, and Howie for being more than just customers at the ULF. My entire family for being there.. Actually, just the family that was there. My aunt Shaheena Haq and her four awesome kids, Furqan, Faizan, Saddef, and Roaida. Love you guys. Thank you naam for all you have done to help us over the years. Thank you nani aman, dadi aman, Afshan khala, Owais uncle, Gurya khala, Salman uncle, Waheed mamoon, Saira khala, Asma khala, Zakir uncle, Rauf mamoon, Tahir mamoon, Nasir mamoon, Riffat aunty, and all. Thank you to all the cousins I haven't seen in so long. I know you are there. Thank you Adnan Rauf for hooking me up with so much awesome music that I could never have gotten anywhere else. Thank you Dr. Pachner and his wonderful staff for keeping me upright for the past ten years.

Thanks Paula for all you do there and, thank you Manica for constantly harassing me about my smoking. But like I always tell you, "mama didn't raise no quitter." And a thank you to my other medical team, Dr. Schriebman, Allyssa Sheridan, and all the great folks at MMH. Yes, I am that sick for having so many people trying to fix me.

I won't mention a name here but I want to thank the love of my life for letting me feel what I wouldn't feel complete without. So you broke my heart and shattered any semblance of trying again. But thank you for letting me know how weak I am when it comes to matters of the heart. You know who you are and I hope you will find your happiness. And I am not being sarcastic. Still love ya. Thank you Michael Rustick for giving a movie geek like me a voice. The Flixter, God willing, shall go on. And I know that you found some of my language in this book objectionable but I have to keep it. I am sorry but its necessary. But thank you SOOO much for being a great friend through my journey. I want to thank my father for making me dread the end of any trip.For making me write about what I had seen and been through. You always told me that writing was very important. Well, abu, I just wrote a whole bunch of stuff. May you rest in peace. Thank you to all the great officers of the KPD for providing security(except for that time the ULF got robbed) and some great friendship.

Thank you Valerie, Paul(Pookie), Kenny, Brian, and all the rest. Thank you to all my teachers through life. All those at Islamabad Model College for Boys. And all those at Roselle Park High School. Mrs. Bilodeau for encouraging me to write and Mrs. Bortnick for still being a friend thirteen years later. Thank you God for being that constant muse who kept me up many nights to fill my head with ideas. Thank you to my music. For providing a soundtrack to my life. All you people from U2 to the Pet Shop Boys. Even the late great Roy Orbison. And thank you Hollywood for letting me live vicariously.Spielberg, Fincher, Koepp, and all. Even those who made junk. If it wasn't for your bad movies, I wouldn't appreciate the good ones. Thank you to The Simpsons for being the best damn thing on TV. It was a tie between you guys and Mystery Science Theater 3000 but that is no more so you win. Thank you to all those who remember me in their thoughts and prayers. Hey, maybe they are working since the Lord may not be so forthright in his giving.

And finally, I want to thank the most courageous, strong, and beautiful person I know. Mom, or Ami as I call her. Thank you for raising me to be what I am. Thank you for instilling the most precious of values in me. Thank you for being you. Love you more than anything.

I.H.